He looked like a Viking

Angie saw him first outlined against the morning sky, and for a moment she caught her breath. He was standing on the deck of a tuna boat, leaning backward against the sky as if he needed no other means of support. Her steps slowed and then stopped, oblivious of everything but the silhouette in front of her.

There was pride in the long, clean lines of his body, strength in the broad shoulders, power in the muscular legs that were planted like tree trunks on the deck. As she drew closer she saw that this Viking had black hair and his skin shone like a new penny in the sun.

A stab of desire, piercing and sweet, coursed through her body. Just for a moment she allowed herself to imagine what it would be like to belong to a man like this . . . in *all* the thrilling secret ways a woman can belong to a man.

Dear Reader,

You're about to behold a "Rising Star!"
Four of them, to be exact. This month, we're
launching into the galaxy of American Romance a
new constellation—the stars of tomorrow... four
authors brand-new to our series.

And they're just in time to celebrate with us the tenth
anniversary of American Romance. In honor of this
occasion, we've got a slew of surprises in store this
year. "Rising Star" is just the beginning!

Join me, then, and welcome Patricia Chandler,
the author of one Superromance title, to
American Romance.

Pat knew that before she could indulge her lifelong
dream of becoming a writer, she had to experience
life. And that's just what she did growing up in San
Diego, where she lived the background to her book.
Listening to the fishermen who mended their nets on
the sidewalk along the waterfront, she knew going to
sea would be the most exciting, romantic life anyone
could live.

Don't wait another minute. Turn the page and catch
a "Rising Star"!

Sincerely,

Debra Matteucci
Senior Editor & Editorial Coordinator
Harlequin
300 East 42nd St.
New York, NY 10017

PATRICIA CHANDLER
AT HER CAPTAIN'S COMMAND

Harlequin Books

TORONTO • NEW YORK • LONDON
AMSTERDAM • PARIS • SYDNEY • HAMBURG
STOCKHOLM • ATHENS • TOKYO • MILAN
MADRID • WARSAW • BUDAPEST • AUCKLAND

With love to my remarkable parents,
Leo and Eileen, the new pioneers

Published August 1993

ISBN 0-373-16497-1

AT HER CAPTAIN'S COMMAND

Prologue

Red sky in the morning, sailor take warning;
Red sky at night, sailor's delight.

Angeli de Vasconceles blinked as her eyes adjusted to
the dim interior of the church. The heavy wooden door
swung shut behind her, blocking out the traffic sounds
from the busy street outside. Automatically she dipped
her fingers into the font of holy water just inside the
vestibule and crossed herself.

Her footsteps echoed hollowly as she walked past the
long rows of pews to the altar, where she genuflected
briefly. Then, turning, she entered a small chapel that
was separated from the nave of the church by somber
red draperies.

The chapel smelled musty—a pungent combination
of incense, wax, pine-tar soap and time. Tiers of vo-
tive candles in blue glass containers were stacked
against the walls. Here and there one burned with a
feeble flame.

In a niche above the candles was a life-size statue of
Saint Andrew, patron saint of fishermen. Gazing
downward, his painted face was sorrowful. His rosy
cheeks and compassionate smile looked like flesh in the

dim light. His smooth, pale hands spread his plaster robes wide, as if to shelter the entire bank of candles.

Angeli took a slip of paper and a pencil stub from a box at the feet of Saint Andrew, and on it she wrote "Jack Reno." Then she held a corner of the paper to one of the burning candles and when it caught, transferred the flame to another, unlighted wick. She dropped the burning scrap into the blue glass holder, where it flared and then curled into glowing ash. For the space of a heartbeat, the flame that had been Jack Reno flickered, and then went out.

She took a second slip of paper and on this one she wrote "Mano de Vasconceles," and with it lit another candle from the first. She held the paper until its tiny flame scorched her fingers, then released it and watched it fall.

The wavering candles threw long shadows on the walls. Saint Andrew's robes seemed to flutter in some unseen current of air that blew through the drafty old church.

Pray for the souls of... The candles guttered fitfully.

Angeli stood with bowed head and face of stone. Her eyes remained fixed on the votives until the glowing scraps of paper had crumbled into cold, gray ash.

Pray for the souls....

At length she turned away from the tiers of blue glass and the empty, painted eyes of the patron saint of fishermen, and stepped back through the heavy red draperies.

Pray....

Chapter One

He always liked making landfall at night. He liked the tiny pinpoints of light that glittered like stars in the hills. He liked watching them magnify, as his boat drew closer, into the tantalizing glow of a city. It must be like being born, he sometimes thought; leaving behind the familiar fluid darkness and moving toward the light— the unknown, beckoning light, where anything could happen, and with a little luck, would.

He guided his boat around the long finger of land called Point Loma, then steered between the buoy markers and followed the ship channel all the way into San Diego Bay.

Beside him on the bridge, his cadaverous-faced first mate turned to eye him with reluctant approval. "Nice piece of work, Captain Callais," he said gruffly.

The captain smiled, both at the formal use of his name and at the grudging tone in his first mate's voice. He wondered with wry humor if the man would have preferred that he'd punched a hole in the pier.

"Come off it, Madruga," he boasted. "You know that was the best damn job of docking you've seen in *your* lifetime!"

"Not bad for a skipper from up along San Pedro, anyway," Madruga conceded. It was a rather heavy-handed attempt at witty repartee, but coming from dour Madruga, the captain knew it was as good as a belly laugh.

He clapped Madruga on the back. "Get below and pack up your gear, man," he ordered jovially. "I'll call you when I get some word on the repairs."

The harbormaster came aboard with his stacks of forms to be signed in triplicate, followed by a contingent of coastguardsmen who ran a team of drug-sniffing dogs through their paces. Then, and only then, was Captain Callais free to shut down the diesels and let his men go home.

"Goin' ashore, Skipper?"

Glancing up, the captain saw his grizzled, gray-haired deckboss standing in the hatchway. The old fisherman had a lumpy seabag slung over one shoulder, and was winded from the exertion of having lugged it up from the fo'c'sle.

"I think not, Dominic."

Dominic gave him a ribald wink. "Lots'a fine entertainment ashore for a young feller like yerself—"

"I think not tonight, Dominic," Captain Callais repeated, returning the old man's lewd grin to show him that his suggestion was nonetheless appreciated.

"Man's gotta eat," Dominic pointed out.

"What?" The captain glanced up again. "Oh, I'll find something in the galley later. I figure I'd better get on these repairs if we're going to catch any fish this season."

"Aint gonna get nothin' done before tomorra," Dominic said with incontestable logic. "Say, why'n't ye come home with me? My old lady dont never mind settin' an extra place at the table fer a feller that's a long way from home.''

"Well, thanks, Dominic. And thank the missus for me, too. I'd like to take you up on that sometime. But for right now—" he gestured toward the multicolored lights and dials of the instrument panel in front of him "—I think I'd better stick around here.''

Dominic raised his bushy gray eyebrows in mute disapproval. Then he shrugged as if to imply it was none of his concern, maneuvered his lumpy seabag into a more comfortable position on his back and shuffled across the gangplank toward the lights on the other side.

With the diesels shut down, the boat was eerily quiet. The sounds of civilization, unheard for so many weeks, drifted into the bridge on the still night air.

The squeal of brakes, the honking of horns. The barking of a dog. Crickets. From a boat moored nearby came the sudden blast of a radio. The voices of passersby floated in from the street, too, as indistinct as whispers by the time they carried across the water.

The sounds were distracting, especially the soft, unfamiliar voices of women. To someone grown accustomed to the company of men, the lilting, honeyed tones were sweet. The women sounded as if they would smell as fragrant as flowers, another thing the captain hadn't experienced in quite a while.

He turned off the computer terminal. With its tiny hum silenced, the sounds of the city became more insistent. They made him feel restless, and that surprised him. Usually there was no place he'd rather be than aboard one of his own vessels.

He went to sea to keep in touch with the fishermen, he told himself, for he was determined never to forget where he'd come from. That sort of hands-on management was the reason for Montero Maritime's meteoric rise to the top, he further told himself, and the reason it would stay there.

But that wasn't the only reason. Simply put, he loved being at sea. He'd loved it since the very first time he'd ever shipped out, at the incredibly green age of fifteen—gangly and awkward, but even then with the long bones and broad shoulders and self-possessed determination that hinted at the man he would someday become.

Everything was exciting then, everything an adventure—so many new things to see and do and taste and feel. He remembered the secret thrill of tying up at some exotic foreign port and wondering, with a gut-wrenching combination of eagerness and apprehension, what awaited him there.

Oh, the women had paled eventually. The all-night drunks and dockside fistfights had faded even sooner than that. And sometimes it seemed that his all-too-brief experiment with domesticity had died the soonest of all.

But the pleasure wasn't only in the arms of women, or in the epic drunks or in the legendary brawls. It was also in the sun and the rain, the scraping of the salt wind like a dull razor against his skin, the pushing of his body to the limit of its endurance, then seeing how much further it could go. The joy was in the living, in the testing of himself against the challenges of a capricious world where most of the variables were unknown.

He sat down in the chair behind the wheel, pivoting it toward the dark expanse of water between himself and the waterfront. Idly he inspected the several re-

flections of his own face that stared back at him from
the windows surrounding the bridge. It was an unusual face. Not much to look at, he thought, the few times
that he thought about it at all. Rough-hewn. Craggy.
Seemingly crafted, not by the chisel of a sculptor, but
by a bricklayer's trowel.

He swiveled the chair back and forth with the toe of
one foot, lit a cigarette, then allowed it to burn forgotten in the corner of his mouth. He should call his office, he reminded himself. Let them know that the *Sea
Witch* had limped safely into the port of San Diego on
her one remaining diesel. He should call his dis-
patcher, Asa Cox, and tell him to start looking for a
new cook on the double.

That was going to present a problem. The great
cooks were reserved years in advance, and this late in
the season the good, and even the merely adequate,
would be taken.

"Damn!" he exclaimed. Tio Leo had been one of the
greats, a legend in the making. What had possessed
him at this stage of his life to set up housekeeping with
a little Panamanian hooker not even old enough to le-
gally drink?

"Damn," he said again, but his voice lacked conviction this time. Instead he smiled, thinking of his
crusty old cook and the childlike girl standing beside
him in her too-short skirt and her too-high heels, with
too much makeup on her round, baby face. And certainly far more optimism in her worldly brown eyes
than the situation warranted.

There'd been something in old Tio Leo's eyes, too—
the triumph of hope over experience, Captain Callais
thought at the time. But he'd also admired the old
man's bullheaded confidence, and he wished the cou-

ple well, even though Tio Leo's impetuous union had left him in a hell of a bind.

The back and forth motion of the chair gradually slowed, then ground to a halt. The captain stubbed out his cigarette in the abalone-shell ashtray at his elbow. His steady gray gaze shifted away from the dark expanse of water and focused instead on the distant halo of lights in the city that circled the harbor.

"THE *SEA WITCH* DOCKED last night."

"Montero's?"

"Who else? They've had a real run of bad luck. Seems their cook quit down in Panama, and the Panamanian they hired to replace him got the D.T.'s a week out and they had to put him ashore. Then no sooner did they get back to the fishing grounds than they ran into heavy seas and lost one of the diesels. I hear they were lucky they even made it home."

"They'll lose weeks! It'll cost them a fortune!"

"Yes."

The two women looked at each other across the small, cluttered office. That they were mother and daughter was indisputable. Both were tall and full-figured. They had the same luxuriant black hair, as glossy as patent leather, the same dark eyes, the same warm olive skin touched high on the cheekbones with the same faint hint of peach.

And just now, the same vivid red lips twisted into the same smiles of grim satisfaction.

"Couldn't happen to a nicer guy!" Angeli de Vasconceles asserted from where she slouched in the depths of a cracked vinyl chair. Her voice was laced with venom. "Who's her skipper, Mom?"

"I didn't recognize the name, Angie. Calley, Kelly, something like that. He's from San Pedro, Dominic told me. You know how those San Pedro men keep to themselves."

"How does Dominic know all this?"

"You haven't heard? He's deckboss on the *Sea Witch.*"

Angie slouched lower on the base of her spine and scowled. "When did he go to work for Montero?"

"When Montero started offering salaries instead of shares," Charlotte Reno replied. "A lot of the men prefer it. Less money in the good seasons, but less risk in the bad. A big-time outfit like Montero's can afford it."

"But *Dominic?*" The hint of peach became an angry crimson flush. "He goes all the way back to Grandfather!"

Charlotte shrugged eloquently. "They aren't *conquistadors* anymore," she reminded her daughter with a small, bitter smile. "Tradition doesn't count for much when there's money to be made. He has his future to consider, and we're certainly not in a position to offer much security right now."

"But. . .*Dominic!* I never thought *he'd* desert us."

"I know, Angie, I know. And I'm counting on you to get him back—him, and the others." Charlotte smiled fondly. "You can't imagine how often I felt like giving up, but I didn't—I knew it would be worth it in the end. And now here you are, the first Reno to graduate from college, and ready to take over. Your father would be proud."

Abruptly mobilizing her various and assorted body parts, Angie hoisted herself out of the sagging chair and sauntered to the window. She peered through the salt-smeared glass at the busy wharf outside, and just beyond, the shimmering turquoise water of San Diego Bay.

Open, closed. She pulled the frayed cord that worked the dusty venetian blinds. Open, closed. College was never something Long Jack Reno wanted for his daughter, but under the circumstances, yes, she supposed he would be proud.

"There's just the one thing, Mom...." Angie began tentatively, still facing the window.

At her back the sudden silence was nerve-racking, and then Charlotte gave an exasperated sigh. "Baby, I thought you'd given that up by now!" From where she sat behind the desk, her voice was as stiff and unyielding as her posture. The ancient watercooler in the corner burbled an equally reproachful rebuke.

"I haven't given it up. I postponed it every time you asked me to, but I've really got to do it now, if I'm ever going to do it at all. Once I get caught up in the business I won't have the time, you know that."

"I simply don't see what you hope to prove by going to sea in the first place. You're not a fisherman, you're an owner...."

"I'm the owner of a fishery that's got no skipper," Angie stated brusquely. "What I hope going to sea will *prove*—" she repeated the word with sharp-tongued emphasis "—is that Reno's isn't going to become one of those fancy corporations like Montero's and WesPac that're only in it for the money."

"Everybody already knows that. Reno's reputation is good."

"Cappy and Grandfather's reputations, you mean. I want the men to know that *we*—you and I—are willing to share the risks as well as the profits. If I can't convince them to give us the same loyalty they gave Cappy, we might just as well pack it in right now."

Charlotte sniffed. "I don't see why you didn't just get your Master's Papers in the first place and be done with it!"

"I considered it." Angie almost smiled, picturing the horrified look on her mother's face. "But I don't think the men are ready for a female skipper, at least not yet. Getting them to accept me as Chief of Operations is going to be enough of a challenge, I think. Besides . . ."

Charlotte caught the hesitation in her daughter's voice. "Besides?" she prodded hopefully, sensing a possible chink in the armor of Angie's stubborn determination.

"I used to love the sea, Mom. I loved it as much as Cappy did. But now I hate it. I wouldn't even make this one last trip if I didn't feel I had to."

"You don't hate the sea, baby. How can you? It's your livelihood."

"I do. I hate it. But worse than that, I'm afraid of it, and I know I can't run Reno's feeling this way. I can't send the boats out season after season, feeling as though I'm condemning the men to certain death!"

"It's dangerous work, of course, but the men know that. They're paid very well to take the risks." Charlotte looked at Angie with eyes that were both fierce and pleading. "The hearing exonerated your father, baby," she said in a low voice. "No one blames us."

"I know that, Mom." Angie turned to face her mother. "It's just *me*. It's just that . . . whenever I read the names on the roster, it's as though it isn't *me* who's reading them. It's Father Ignacio, calling them out in Portuguese Hall—'Pray for the souls of . . .'"

She shuddered. She knew the names by heart. She had heard them all her life on Pentecost, *Espiritu Santu,* the Day of the Dead. *Jesu Amacar... Will Antonio...Kenneth Bonfiglioli....* They ran through her memory like the singsong verses of a child's nursery rhyme, an alphabetical litany of names that had no significance other than the fact that they belonged to men who had been lost at sea. And new names every year. *Mano de Vasconceles. Jack Reno.*

"The thing is... the thing is, I've lost so much, baby." Charlotte's voice rose precariously. "Your father. Mano. The thing is... I just couldn't bear it... if it was *your* name Father Ignacio read out in Portuguese Hall."

Angie's chin trembled as she turned back to the window, unable for the moment to meet her mother's eyes. She pulled the frayed cord of the blinds. Open, closed. Open, closed. "I'm sorry, Mother," she said finally. "I don't like to hurt you."

The voice behind her took on a brisk, businesslike tone. "Well, I'm afraid it's just impossible this year. I've already hired four full crews. Maybe next year—"

"Mother!" Angie whirled angrily. "We agreed!"

"We agreed on nothing. This is business, baby. You know I can't let something like that go until the last minute. I don't want to end up with four boats full of men no one else wanted." Charlotte busied herself with the invoices on her desk. "Maybe next year...." she repeated.

"Next year will be too late, Mother. You know that."

"I know it. In fact, I'm counting on it." Charlotte pulled her reading glasses from her face and tossed them onto the desk. "You may as well understand,

Angie," she said, tiredly massaging the bridge of her nose with thumb and forefinger, "that you will never go to sea on a Reno vessel. Not while I have anything to say about it."

Mother and daughter glowered at each other. Charlotte dropped her eyes first. "You look just like your father," she muttered, "standing there glaring at me that way."

"I don't want to hurt you, Mom," Angie said again, more gently this time. "But I need this one last time. *Reno's* needs this one last time."

"There's really no point to this discussion. The boats are full. Surely you wouldn't want me to let one of the men go, someone who's probably got a wife and children to support, just on some whim of yours?"

Angie studied her mother. Charlotte's head was bent over the papers on her desk, acting for all the world as though the issue had been settled. Abruptly Angie turned and jerked open the door.

"You should have waited, Mom. You really should have waited." She pulled the door shut behind her with just the suggestion of a slam and stepped out into the thin yellow of the afternoon sun.

Hands jammed into her pockets, she strode to the edge of the wharf and looked down at the water lapping against the pilings. The somber eyes of her own reflection stared back at her from the oily surface. *Twenty-eight years old and still drifting with the tide,* they seemed to taunt her. *Twenty-eight years old and still . . . unanchored.*

Cappy! she thought rebelliously, jutting out her own chin in unconscious imitation of her father's stubborn lantern jaw. Cappy would understand.

The reckless Long Jack had never let himself become hidebound by tradition. He had ignored the amused glances that had followed him when he practically raised his young daughter on the docks. He had only laughed at the shock waves that reverberated through the Portuguese neighborhood when he took her halfway around the world as cook on Reno's flagship, his old *Mackerel Sky*. And he was inordinately proud of the fact that she was as skilled with the nets as she was with a skillet.

But even Long Jack had a traditional streak that surfaced at the most unexpected times. There had been a Reno at the head of Reno Fisheries since his own father—at the time, a greenhorn barely out of his teens and fresh from the Azores—had founded it over half a century ago. Long Jack, lacking a son, had counted instead on a son-in-law, or on an eventual grandson to take over the business. He had never foreseen a time when the operation of Reno Fisheries would fall on the unprepared shoulders of his only daughter.

But that time had come. Cappy was dead; his son-in-law was dead. There had never been a grandson, and Charlotte ran Reno's now.

A lot of things had changed in the four years since Charlotte had taken over, and they would have changed no matter who had been at the helm of Reno Fisheries. Most of the smaller companies were in trouble, struggling to stay afloat in the face of competition from large, aquabusiness conglomerates. And one such conglomerate, Montero Maritime, out of San Pedro, was after Reno's.

Montero Maritime—a cheeky upstart that had only amused Long Jack ten years ago. *I took Montero out the first time he ever went to sea. Too serious for a kid.*

But hardworking. Well, he wouldn't laugh anymore. Montero had bought out most of the smaller fisheries in San Pedro, and now he was trying to extend his influence into San Diego.

But, armed with her business degree, hard-won by a former Portuguese princess who had never been expected to excel in anything as unimportant as schoolwork, Angie intended to take on Montero's. And she intended to win.

But there was another battle she had to win first. First she had to resolve the strange love-hate ambivalence toward the sea that had festered inside her since Cappy's death. The sea was her heritage. It was in her blood on both sides of her family as far back as anyone could remember. She had taken her first staggering steps on the boards of Long Jack's old *Mackerel Sky.* That was the love.

Then there was Della Araujo, her best friend since childhood, whose mother was Angie's godmother and whose father, God have mercy on his soul, had been her godfather.

Indelibly etched in Angie's mind was the image of a wide-eyed little girl of seven, so solemn, concentrating so hard on doing everything exactly right. It was Della's first time, that *Espiritu Santu* so long ago, but she didn't even cry when Father Ignacio called her father's name and she threw her small handful of flowers into the bay. Angie used to wonder how it felt not to have a father anymore.

And that was the hate.

Hands still jammed in her pockets, Angie slouched moodily along the waterfront, past the sagging, timeworn warehouses that seemed to lean against one another for support. She stopped in front of one nondescript brown building and realized, with some surprise, that she had intended to come here all along. A tarnished bronze plaque beside the door said simply Montero Maritime.

Chapter Two

"Can't do it, Angie. Your mother would cut my heart out."

"My mother has nothing to do with it. Can I do the work or not?"

Behind his thick spectacles, Asa Cox's watery blue eyes were distressed. He retreated behind the relative safety of his desk. "That's not the point. A girl like you..."

"Women sign on tuna boats all the time."

"Sure, but not women like you. Older, able to take care of themselves. You know what I'm saying...."

"I was sixteen the first time I shipped out. You know I can take care of myself. And you know I can cook, Asa, and you need a cook. I can lend a hand with the nets, too."

"All I know is your daddy took you out a couple of summers, but you were just a kid. It was a game you and Long Jack played. It wasn't anything like the real thing."

"I can do the job, Asa. And I *need* to do it." Angie hesitated. "There are some...ghosts...that I need to lay to rest."

"Wish I could help you, kid."

Angie realized that her arguments were falling on deaf ears. Asa was implacable, and he had centuries of tradition to back him up. To her great humiliation, tears of frustration welled up in her eyes.

Asa's Adam's apple bobbed convulsively. "Angie!" he wailed. "C'mon, don't do that!"

Long Jack's *son,* if he'd had a son, wouldn't embarrass himself or his father this way, Angie berated herself. A son would blurt something succinct and graphic, undoubtedly in Portuguese, undoubtedly profane, exactly as Long Jack himself would have done.

Mentally she sorted through her own stock of colorful epithets. Finding none sufficiently satisfying for this particular occasion, she instead executed a sharp about-face on the heel of her sneaker, which made a gratifying squeak that sounded like the scraping of fingernails across a blackboard. She jerked open the door and flung herself through the doorway....

...And headlong into the arms of the tall man who stood by the reception desk. He staggered backward, automatically catching her in his arms as he struggled to keep his balance. Angie found herself staring into the startled gray eyes of a total stranger, a stranger whose arms were wrapped around her as intimately as a lover's.

She was tall, but he was taller, and the accidental touch of his body along the full length of hers made her feel at once small and vulnerable. It was not a feeling she had experienced in her life, but one that she found unexpectedly pleasurable.

That he was a fisherman she could tell immediately. He smelled of cold seawater and faintly of fish, with a fainter odor of diesel fuel and the barest suggestion of a musky after-shave. And he must have just come in from the boats, because he was still wearing a yellow oilskin slicker and bulky seaboots turned down at the tops.

A nimbus of flyaway hair, vibrant with a life of its own, curled around her head, tickling the tall fisherman's chin, sending sensations like tiny electric shocks clear down to his toes. The electricity was the first thing he felt. He also felt and appreciated every voluptuous curve of the lush body that had nearly decked him.

He kept his arms around her a moment longer than was strictly necessary, then regretfully released her. He saw that she had been crying. What could mild-mannered Asa have said or done, he wondered, to provoke this kind of response?

"Easy there," he said good-naturedly. "You okay?"

"S-sorry," Angie stammered unsteadily. "I was just... I was... I..." She straightened her collar, ran her fingers quickly over her cheeks, lightly smoothed her frizzled hair. Then, backing up a few inches, she produced an awkward and embarrassed smile. "Sorry," she repeated self-consciously.

Smiling down into her face, his eyes, gleaming like pewter and narrowed as though facing perpetually into the wind, narrowed even more. "Have we...met?" he asked, looking a bit unsettled himself.

Impossible! he answered his own question, for every instinct told him that if he had ever set eyes on her before, he surely would not have forgotten.

Still backing toward the door, Angie shook her head.

"Goodbye, Mrs. de Vasconceles," the receptionist sang out brightly. "You may go in now," she said, turning to the tall fisherman.

The puzzled expression still on his face, he stepped across the tiny reception room to open the outside door for Angie. He watched her take the stairs two at a time, then stride away with a long-legged, mannish gait that was, on her, bewitchingly feminine.

"You may go in now, Captain Callais," the receptionist repeated with bureaucratic impatience, swiveling around in her chair. She saw, with a touch of irritation, that the tall fisherman had already disappeared into Asa's private office.

"Who was that?" Joseph Callais asked, draping his long body on a corner of Asa's desk.

"That? Oh, that was Angeli Reno."

"So *that's* Angie Reno," Joseph said, as much to himself as to Asa. "Of course. I should have figured. Looks just like her mother." He stared strangely at the door through which Angie had just disappeared.

Asa harrumphed cryptically. "Looks like her mother, right enough, but she's got her daddy's temper. For a minute there I thought it was old Long Jack himself standing right here in my office, giving me what for!"

Joseph cocked a quizzical eyebrow. "What was she doing here?"

"You'll love this, Joe. Looking for a job."

"What job?"

"Cook. On the *Sea Witch*." Asa snorted. "Can you believe it? Even if she *didn't* look like that, I'd never take her on. She's bad luck. After what happened to her husband and her daddy, I doubt I could get a crew to sail with her. She says she has some ghosts to lay to rest. Not on one of my boats, she doesn't!"

"Your secretary called her something else."

"De Vasconceles? Yeah, that's her married name. Got a new girl on the desk—doesn't know Angie like the rest of us. Hell, Long Jack practically *raised* her on these docks. She'll never be anything but little Angie Reno to us."

Asa *tsk tsk'd* fondly. "Yeah, you never saw old Long Jack but that he had little Angie up on his shoulders. Never saw a man carry on over a kid the way he did over that one. Yeah, old Long Jack—you knew him?"

"I knew him. She's married?"

"Not anymore she isn't."

"Divorced, then?" Joseph's voice was impatient, but Asa Cox was not one to make a long story short.

"Divorced? Angie Reno? After the biggest wedding Tunaville's ever seen? With the bishop himself doing the honors? Not bloody likely! No, she's a widow, Angie is. Mano de Vasconceles, that was her husband. Yeah, Mano, God rest his soul...." Asa reached down surreptitiously to rap his knuckles on the drawer of his wooden desk. "He went down with her father out in the North Atlantic, four years ago."

Joseph drummed his fingers on top of the desk. His dark face was thoughtful. "Hire her," he said finally.

"But, Joe!" Asa gulped, his bulging eyes and the shocked O of his pursed mouth making him look rather like a hooked fish himself. "Didn't I just tell you? She's bad luck! We've had trouble enough on the *Sea Witch!* Her on top of everything else, we're likely to have a mutiny on our hands!"

"Can she do the work?"

"Can she—? She's a big girl. Of course she can do the work. That's not the point!"

"She's an Amazon," Joseph said briefly. "Hire her."

"Aw, Joe," Asa wailed. "Why?"

"Simple. I need a cook."

Asa snorted disbelievingly.

"All right, then. I want Reno's. I've been trying to deal with Charlotte Reno for years and gotten nowhere. If I can convince Mrs. de Vasconceles that she'd be better off out of the business, maybe she'll be able to influence her mother.

"Women don't belong in the tuna fleet, Asa. No matter how the men felt about Long Jack, there's no way they're going to accept a woman's lead, you know that. I think it's time Mrs. de Vasconceles learned it, too."

"What're you going to do?" Asa asked apprehensively.

"Me? I'm not going to do a thing. Just being out at sea on a tuna boat that's not her father's will do it all, I think. She'll hate it, and maybe that'll be the wedge I need."

"Her daddy was a friend of mine. . . ." Asa began.

"He was a friend of mine, too, in a way. He was the first skipper I ever sailed under. Taught me to love the sea the way he did. Taught me to respect it. You don't have to worry, Asa. My intentions are strictly honorable." Joseph stood to leave, his face still thoughtful.

"You're the boss, Joe," Asa said, spreading his hands, palms upward, in a placating gesture. "You don't owe me any explanations."

"I know I don't, but you were a friend of Long Jack's, so I figure you have a right to know. Reno's was in trouble even before Long Jack went down, and without him they haven't got a prayer. We both know they're going to have to sell, sooner or later. It might as well be now. And it might as well be me. I'll give them a fair price, and that's more than anyone else will do, knowing the mess they're in.''

"There's been Reno's in San Diego for over half a century," Asa reflected sadly. "It's really too bad."

Joseph shrugged. "It's a new age, Asa. You change with the times or you get left behind." He started to leave, but at the door he paused, back still to the room, and propped his arm against the doorjamb.

"One more thing," he said, not turning around. "I'm not from around these parts, but I'm fairly certain the residents of Point Loma don't appreciate hearing their lovely neighborhood referred to as 'Tunaville.'"

"Sure, Joe, whatever you say. I didn't mean anything by it. Even the Port-a-gee call it that—"

But Asa's explanation was cut short by the decisive click of the closing door.

AS ANGIE SAW IT, an evening with Georgie Correia no longer qualified as a date. It was more along the order of a board meeting. She sat with him in the penthouse lounge of one of the most exclusive restaurants in town. A single red candle gave their tiny booth an intimate glow.

Georgie was an attorney for WesPac, a large fishery that aspired to conglomerate status. From his close-cropped, sandy hair to the high gloss on his wing tips, Georgie was more urbane than most of the men Angie knew. Sometimes she thought of him as sophisticated; tonight, the word that occurred to her most often was *slick*.

Often she wondered what attracted him more—her, or the possibility of buying out Reno Fisheries?

"I agree with Asa Cox. Women don't belong on tuna boats." Behind his rimless glasses Georgie's pale eyes registered disapproval. "Especially not women like you." He flashed her his most charming smile. "Have I told you how pretty you look tonight?"

Angie frowned. "Don't start that, Georgie," she warned, fidgeting self-consciously with the lapel of her tailored silk shirt. "It's just an old tweed suit that I've had forever."

Pretty? Hers was a face that launched a thousand ships, Cappy used to say, long before she had ever heard of Helen of Troy. In those agonizing teen years, when she had shot up taller than any of the boys and more buxom than any of the girls, she had longed for the pert features and trim figure of a cheerleader, and had despaired the classic symmetry of a face that was out-of-date, and a body that belonged on the prow of a ship.

Pretty? She picked up her glass and tossed what was left of the wine down her throat with one abrupt gesture, in much the same way Long Jack used to drain a glassful of beer in a single long swallow. Then, coughing, she returned the goblet to the table with a force that threatened the fragile stem. No, whatever else she might be, she knew she wasn't pretty. She had long since learned to live with that.

"I fail to see why you can't accept a simple compliment without an argument," Georgie complained. "Why don't you cut me a little slack, babe? Who knows, I might grow on you. After all, we could end up doing business together."

"You're wasting your time, Georgie, and so is WesPac." This was familiar ground, and more comfortable to Angie than the murky quagmire of relationships where she was never quite confident of the terrain. "Your people suck the life out of every fishery they buy up. No money is ever put back into the boats—it just goes to redecorate your corporate offices. Before I'd sell to WesPac I'd dismantle every boat and sell it for scrap!"

"Well, it's us or Montero's." Georgie smirked. "And they're even bigger than we are." He spoke with the supercilious tone Angie so disliked. "Your options have narrowed considerably."

"I hate Montero's and everything it stands for, but I have to admit it's got the best safety record in the fleet. WesPac doesn't even come close. Don't look so smug, Georgie. We're going to turn Reno's around, my mother and I—"

"Ah, yes, your mother. A difficult woman. She would have saved herself and you a lot of grief if she'd sold when we made our first offer." He twirled his wineglass between manicured fingers. "You and I both know that you're overextended. It was a bad business decision to put all that new electronic gear on your boats—"

"After what happened, she couldn't let the men go out with less than the best," Angie said defensively. "And neither could I. You must understand that."

"What *I* understand is that you couldn't afford it. And now, if your boats do as badly as they did last year, you won't even be able to make the interest payments on your loans."

Angie stared at him, dumbfounded.

"I see you didn't know that. What else do you think Charlotte's not telling you? The best thing you can do, for your mother *and* yourself, is to get out and let someone take over the operation who knows how to run it."

"You."

"WesPac. We can salvage Reno's now. Soon it'll be too late."

Georgie studied the impotent fury on Angie's face. Upon hearing her tight "I'd like to leave now," he realized unhappily that he had pushed her too far. Again.

ONCE INSIDE the stately old Victorian that had been the Reno home for three generations, Angie ran up the stairs to her own bedroom. There, pinned to her pillow, was a message from Fatima, the Reno's ancient housekeeper, who was almost as old as the house itself. "Call Asa Cox."

Chapter Three

She saw him first outlined against the morning sky, and for a moment she caught her breath.

He was standing on the deck of a tuna boat, leaning backward against the sky as if he needed no other means of support. Angie's steps slowed and then stopped, oblivious of everything but the silhouette in front of her.

There was pride in the long, clean lines of his body, and strength in the broad shoulders. And there was power in the muscular legs that were planted like tree trunks on the deck. His back was to the sun and Angie couldn't see his face, but somehow she knew instinctively that he would be smiling.

He looked like a Viking; but as she drew closer, she saw that this Viking had black hair, not blond, and his skin shone like a new penny in the sun. *A conquistador* then—Charlotte's word for those brave, arrogant men who explored the world for their kings, and peopled it with their Latin seed.

As she moved closer, the name of the boat came into view. *Sea Witch.* And the silhouette of the *conquistador* took on the features of a man. It was the tall fisherman from Asa's office the day before. He was mending nets—standing astride the enormous net pile, feeding the thick twine through his hands and feeling for tears with strong, sensitive fingers.

"Hello!" Angie hailed, one hand raised to her eyes against the sun. "I'm looking for the skipper."

The fisherman motioned her aboard. She crossed the gangplank and jumped to the deck, then walked aft to where he stood with his nets. "You must be our new cook." Holding on to a cable with one hand, he extended the other down to her. "Joseph—"

"Angeli," she replied, shaking the proffered hand.

In the bright sunlight, he wasn't as young as he had first appeared, but of course it was impossible to judge a fisherman's age. After a few years at sea, they all looked alike—eyes squinted as if perpetually facing into the wind, skin tanned like leather, lines carved as though in stone.

This man's face was like that. It was made of angles—a square jaw and triangular cheekbones, bisected by parallel slashes of mouth and brows. There was a cleft in the chin that looked almost like a scar. Angie saw at once that it was not a face many would find attractive; she decided that she liked it very much.

He hunkered down on his heels and grinned at her. "Do I pass?"

"Oh, I'm sorry! It's just that you... remind me of someone." *I know you. I've always known you.* Then it came to her. He looked like Cappy. Cappy, the way he had appeared to her when she was a child—young and handsome. Reckless. Immortal.

Vaulting down from the net pile, he stood before her on the deck and gave her a thorough once-over from behind his sunglasses. His grin broadened. "May I say that your reputation preceded you? And may I also say that it's well deserved?''

Angie felt a secret muscle coil somewhere in the vicinity of her stomach. She knew she ought to be offended by his impudent appraisal, which he made no attempt to hide. Instead she found herself hoping he approved of what he saw.

''You may say it if you like,'' she replied, in a voice that was uncharacteristically flirtatious. ''But I really don't know what you mean.''

''Angiereno. That's how people say it around here. One word. Crown princess of Reno Fisheries. Only child of Long Jack Reno. Probably—no, definitely—the loveliest cook to ever grace the boards of a tuna boat. Or any other boat, for that matter.''

The compliment didn't make her squirm uncomfortably, as such observations normally did. ''That's very kind of you,'' she said simply.

''Now signing on with her archenemy, Montero. Why?''

''Fair question. But one I think only the skipper has the right to ask.''

''Of course.''

''What's he like, the skipper?''

''Oh, he's all right, I guess.''

''I mean, what's he like to work under? What do the men think of him?''

Joseph shrugged. ''Hard to say. Doesn't talk much. Just your average, run-of-the-mill skipper, I guess. Company man.''

An unconscious note of derision crept into Angie's voice. ''More concerned with the profits than with the men, that kind of company man?''

"Well, I don't know about that. A company doesn't get far by disregarding its men. Tunamen are a pretty independent lot, I'm sure you know that."

"I know that they lose a lot of their independence when they sign on with a big-time outfit like Montero's. You, for example. Wouldn't you like to own a boat of your own instead of—"

"Skipper!" shouted a voice from the lower deck.

Joseph turned. "What d'ye need, chief?"

"'Nother twenty minutes, we can give that number-two diesel a try!"

"Be right with you." He turned his attention back to Angie. "You were saying...?" he said courteously.

"You're the skipper," she croaked in a strangled voice.

"That's right."

"You should have identified yourself!"

"What? And missed your trying to incite me to mutiny? Not on your life!"

It was difficult to resist the half-dozen or so sharp retorts that leapt to the tip of her tongue, but common sense prevailed. They would only make matters worse, and he seemed to be enjoying her discomfiture far too much already.

"I'm sorry, sir. I was out of line."

"You were," he agreed pleasantly.

"It won't happen again, I assure you. I'd like to thank you for giving me this opportunity—"

"So you're Angie Reno."

"De Vasconceles, sir," she corrected.

"Yes, of course. De Vasconceles. You're almost as much of a legend in the fleet as your father, did you know that?"

Obviously not expecting an answer, he paced back and forth, hands behind his back as if he were conducting an interrogation. "So you want to cook on the *Sea Witch?*" he said finally. "How do you know we need one?"

"Everyone knows, sir. The scuttlebutt is you got a bad start to the season."

"Yes, well, what are they saying about us? Calling us a bad-luck vessel, no doubt."

"No, sir, not exactly."

"It's a little late for you to start being diplomatic, don't you think? No one is sorry to see—what did you call us?—*a big-time outfit* like Montero's in trouble."

"Everyone is sorry to see any boat in trouble, sir. The men—most of them are related in one way or another. If one boat suffers, all the families suffer. At least, that's the way it is in San Diego." She couldn't keep a touch of malice out of her voice. "I don't know what it's like up along San Pedro."

He was silent for so long that she wondered if the interview, such as it was, was terminated. "And you?" he continued finally, the question thrown at her so abruptly that she jumped. "Why are you looking for a berth so late in the season? No one else'd have you?"

"No, sir. I was away. I thought it was all arranged, but when I came back I found that it wasn't, and all the other boats were full. But I'm good. I'll do a good job for you. I'm sure Asa Cox told you that—"

"You were available," the skipper interrupted bluntly. "And you were cheaper than getting an experienced cook down from San Pedro, that's all. If I'd had any choice, I wouldn't have hired a woman."

"Well, then, I'll have to thank Asa for giving me the chance to prove myself. He won't be sorry, sir. And neither will you."

The skipper ignored her conciliatory words. "Where were you that you neglected to assure yourself of a job for the season?"

"I was away at college, sir."

"College?" He sounded surprised. "No one told me you were a college student."

"I'm not anymore. I graduated last week."

"Now why would a college graduate want to work on a tuna boat?" he demanded in honest confusion.

The "why," Angie thought, wasn't important, except to her. "Why *wouldn't* a college graduate want to work on a tuna boat? It's honest work."

"It is. But you don't spend four years in college preparing for it." He regarded her thoughtfully. "What did you study?"

"Business."

"Business?" His face cleared and he gave a loud and, to Angie's ears, offensive *"Hah!* Business! I should have figured!" Still chuckling, he returned to the net pile and sprinted to the top of the seven-foot heap.

"Go find the galley," he called down to Angie. "See what you want by way of supplies, then go get a chit from Asa for the commissary. And, hey! Just because we're a *big-time outfit,* don't think you're on an unlimited expense account!"

He turned his back and resumed what he had been doing when she arrived. It was hard and tedious work, mending nets, but he made it appear effortless. Covertly she watched him, noticing the efficient interplay of muscle beneath the blue chambray as he hoisted the twine and fed it through his hard, brown fingers.

What was he made of, Angie wondered, this Joseph—Calley, or Kelly or whatever name it was that Dominic had told Charlotte? A little arrogant, a bit too cocksure, maybe, but those were not undesirable traits in a skipper, not if they were properly balanced with knowledge and skill. And not the type, she suspected, to be content working for someone else forever.

She filed his name away in the back of her mind for future reference and went to check out the galley.

AFTER DETERMINING WHAT she needed to replenish her provisions, Angie stopped at Montero's warehouse. Asa Cox was not in a receptive mood.

"Don't thank me," he growled. "It was him, Captain Callais, that did it."

"I don't understand."

"He's the skipper. If it'd been up to me, well, I wouldn't have taken you on. I like you, Angie. For old times' sake—for *Long Jack's* sake!—I wish you'd reconsider."

"And what would you do for a cook, Asa, if I did reconsider? I'm cheaper than getting a cook down from San Pedro—the skipper himself told me so. I'm a bargain, Asa!"

"Bargain!" Asa snorted under his breath, then dropped his voice to a conspiratorial whisper. "Just between you and me, Angie girl, there's things here you don't know anything about. This skipper—"

This skipper. She saw him again as she had seen him that morning—the sun at his back, his silhouette filling up the morning sky. Not many skippers mended their own nets. Cappy did.

And like Cappy, it was obvious that this skipper wasn't afraid to take risks. Angie knew that among the superstitious fishermen, there were some who regarded her as *mav sorte*—bad luck—and there was always the chance that some of the crew would refuse to sail with her, leaving the *Sea Witch* shorthanded for the season.

All in all, this skipper had gone out on a limb for her, Angie reminded herself. He could use her if he chose; after all, she was certainly using him.

"All I need to know," Angie interrupted, "is whether he's good at his job. And I figure he must be, or Montero's wouldn't have given him his own boat, right? I already *know* he's not a *nice* guy. What *nice* guy would be working for an outfit like Montero's? Well, except you, of course, Asa."

With wry affection she patted his bony shoulder. "Don't worry about me. I can take care of myself. And none of your crew is going to come back with any complaints, I guarantee."

Conflicting loyalties were evident in Asa's face. "Just watch yourself, Angie girl" was all he finally said.

"Hey, what is this skipper, some kind of Captain Ahab or something? Whatever his game is, I'll turn it around and beat him at it. Just you wait and see!"

Asa was plainly doubtful.

THE WATERFRONT WAS shrouded by fog. A drizzling mist, too fine to be called rain, made the concrete wharf slick and treacherous.

Beside the *Sea Witch*'s gangplank, Angie, outfitted in yellow oilskin and sou'wester, struggled with a stack of heavy cartons. For some reason known only to God and the delivery boy, the commissary supplies she ordered had been dumped at the foot of the Market Street pier, and it was left up to her to get them across the gangplank and aboard the *Sea Witch* as best she could.

Unable to lift one particularly heavy carton, she was backing up the wet gangplank, pulling the box along in front of her.

"I thought you'd done this kind of work before."

Angie whirled, releasing the carton, which proceeded to slide back down the gangplank and topple onto the wharf. In the shadow of the upper deck stood the skipper, leaning backward with one foot propped against the bulkhead and his arms folded across his chest. He looked as though he had been standing there for some time.

He wore an oilskin identical to the one Angie was wearing, and a cigarette dangled loosely from the corner of his mouth. He pushed himself away from the bulkhead and flicked the cigarette over the side, then edged past Angie to the bottom of the gangplank.

"Push it," he called up to her, as he lifted the box back on the ramp. "Throw your back into it. Like this." Effortlessly the carton slid up the ramp and tumbled onto the deck. "That shouldn't be hard, big girl like you."

Angie scowled at him. "Thanks. I'll remember."

"Of course, a *man* would have known that." He balanced with one foot on the rail, then stepped down to the deck. "This is a real working boat, Reno, not a cruise ship. I expect you to pull your own weight."

She folded her lips over angry words. "Well, if you'll excuse me, then," she said frostily, "I have work to do."

"Take a break. You look like you could use one. Any coffee in the galley?"

"I think so."

"Want to make me a cup?"

"Is that an order, Skipper?"

He grinned engagingly, his teeth very white in his dark, leathered face. "Only if it has to be." Draping an affable arm around Angie's shoulders, he propelled her through the hatch that led to the galley.

The supplies she had carted aboard were stacked everywhere. Angie removed her damp oilskin and dragged the sou'wester from her head, and tossed them both across a pile of boxes. She suspected that, in spite of the sou'wester, the mist had frizzed her hair into an unruly mop; she had no idea why the knowledge disturbed her so much. "Now," was all she said aloud, "where's the coffee?"

"First shelf, far left cupboard."

"Thanks."

"Mugs, middle left, over the booze locker."

He knows his way around a galley, she thought with grudging approval. "A good skipper knows every inch of his vessel," Cappy used to say.

When the coffee was heated, Angie poured it into two thick, white mugs and placed one in front of the skipper where he sat at the only cleared spot on the table. "I hope you take it black," she said. "I have no idea where the sugar is, unless—" she glanced at him inquiringly "—you do."

"Black's fine." The mug disappeared into his big hands as he lifted it to his lips. "Good coffee. Strong."

She smiled reluctantly, surprised at the pleasure the offhand compliment gave her. "I remembered—that's the way my father liked it."

"And your husband? Did he like it that way, too?"

The smile vanished. "Yes," she said briefly. "But why that should concern you..."

"Everything that happens aboard this boat concerns me." He regarded her with narrow, inscrutable eyes. "You, of all people, should know that. If I'm going to have a morale problem a week out, I'd rather know it now."

"You'll have no morale problems with me, Skipper. I can assure you of that. I know what I'm doing."

"Do you? I wonder. This is a tuna boat, Reno. It's full of men who live their lives without women. We're sure to be a little...*rough*...around the edges. We can be crude, and there are bound to be times when we forget there's a lady on board. I'm not even sure we should be expected to remember."

"It's your world, you mean. I'm the outsider."

"Outsider. Yes. I'm glad you understand that." Across the table, his yellow oilskin hung open, revealing the dungarees and blue chambray work shirt that were practically the uniform of tunamen—except in the tropics, where it became shorts and sunglasses.

Reluctantly, Angie's eyes were drawn to the muscled thighs encased in the faded denim. His legs were crossed, the ankle of one propped on the knee of the other. It was a very provocative pose; she wondered if he knew that.

Her glance traveled lower, to the triangle of wooden chair she could see between the V of his legs; then still lower, to the hand that rested just above one knee. It was broad and brown. There were calluses on the palm, and a bruise at the base of the thumb.

The hand of a workingman. A strong hand. Tiny hairs tufted on the back of the tanned wrist, and disappeared into the cuff of his shirt. They looked crisp and springy, and Angie wondered suddenly how they would feel, springing to life against the palm of her hand.

For a dizzying instant, she saw nothing but that suntanned hand: the curling dark hair, the strength implicit in the cordlike tendons and in the powerful thigh where it rested. Something hot and sweet stirred inside her. Angie shifted uncomfortably in her chair. *Is it really as simple as that? Is that all you need?*

Maybe it was only because he looked a little like Mano, sitting across the table in his work clothes, the way she had seen Mano sit so often in the few short years of their marriage. Maybe it was because he seemed so capable and solid and self-assured. Or maybe, she admitted more frankly, it was simply that he looked as though he would know how to handle a woman. She shifted again.

"...And get your goodbyes said," the skipper's voice was advising her, as he withdrew a cigarette from the pack in his breast pocket and inserted it between his lips. He patted the rest of his pockets until he found his lighter and held it to the tip of the cigarette, cupping his palm around the flame from long habit as if to shield it from the wind.

"We sail with the tide on Saturday," he continued between puffs. "Check in with the watch before 2400 hours Friday."

He scraped his chair back from the table and stood to leave. "And, Reno...?"

"Yes, sir?"

"Welcome aboard."

Chapter Four

The air was thick with the smell of wet lumber and rotting fish, and gritty with the taste of salt and sand. Lights were beginning to come on in the sleeping city— tiny pinpoints that only weakly pierced the leaden fog.

Angie stood at the rail, surveying the rain-drenched wharf. Her yellow oilskin was the only bright spot in the otherwise colorless landscape.

Down on the waterfront, she could see a derelict curled up on a bench, trying to catch a few hours' sleep before a squad car rousted him. Another derelict, collar turned up against the chill, picked through a trash can on the quay. Gulls shrieked and circled low, searching for bits of flotsam brought in by the tide.

At the foot of Market Street, a group of people huddled together, looking like a cluster of mushrooms under the umbrellas that concealed their faces. It was the same small gathering that usually came to see a tuna boat off—mostly women, although there were also a few children, and from somewhere beneath the umbrellas a baby's thin wail drifted upward.

It was a depressing scene, Angie thought, as these middle-of-the-night leave-takings always were. She wondered why she had even bothered to come topside.

Suddenly her attention was riveted by a figure standing some distance from the others, alone under a streetlight. Wrapped in a familiar gray raincoat, crowned by a familiar hat with the brim pulled low, the figure was only a little darker than the gray dawn that surrounded it, but Angie knew instantly who it was. There was no mistaking the regal height, the elegant lift of the head, the ramrod straight posture. Her mother had come to see her off.

Angie was surprised. Charlotte hadn't gone to one of Cappy's departures for many years. It was considered, if not exactly bad luck, at least unnecessary. The boats went out, and in two or three or four months they came back; there was no point in tempting the Fates by suggesting that there might be any question about it.

Angie waved at the motionless statue that was Charlotte. The slanted gray hat tilted upward as Charlotte waved back, giving Angie a glimpse of pale face and wide, haunted eyes under the stark glare of the streetlight.

Did her mother regret not having seen Cappy off on that last voyage? Angie wondered. A clammy shiver raced up her spine. Someone just walked over my grave, she thought uneasily. She fought the almost irresistible urge to cross herself as her *avó*, old Grandmother Reno, had always done when saying those words. She shivered again.

The foghorn on the point gave a long, plaintive moan like the melancholy lowing of a cow; the sound skirted the harbor, echoing hollowly. Then the *Sea Witch* responded with her own horn, indicating she was ready to get underway.

The boat lumbered starboard, then port, and finally entered the ship channel. The pier slowly receded. Soon even the magnificent skyline became nothing more than a smudge against the lightening sky. But not until the *Sea Witch* had rounded the long finger of Point Loma and headed for the open sea did Angie turn away from the rail.

. . . And collided with a wall that hadn't been there before. She caught her breath. "That's the second time you've tried to run me down, Reno!" said the wall in a good-natured voice that nevertheless made Angie's heart sink. "Couldn't you arrange to use turn signals or something?"

"Certainly, Skipper," she retorted snappishly. "Or you could arrange to stop sneaking up behind me like that!"

"I paged you," the skipper protested, the amused tone still in his voice. "You were a million miles away."

He turned toward the shore, propping his elbows on the rail, and gazed at San Diego Bay as it disappeared around Point Loma. For just a moment the sun broke through the gray sky, washing the receding landscape in pale lavender, and touching the serrated peaks of the skyscrapers with gold.

"Take a good look," the skipper said softly, almost as though speaking to himself. "It'll be a long time before you see it again." Then he quirked one eyebrow quizzically at Angie. "Anyone come to see you off? A boyfriend? Your mother, maybe?"

Certainly not a boyfriend. Georgie might continue to press for the acquisition of Reno's for WesPac, but Angie doubted whether his interest would ever again be anything more than purely professional. Not after the quarrel they'd had the night before.

At first he hadn't believed she really meant to go; then his disbelief had turned into hurt, and finally had become humiliation. "What will people think?" he'd objected angrily. "Everyone knows how I feel about you, and now here you are, going out on a boat full of men, like . . . like a . . ."

"Like a what?" Angie had demanded, but Georgie couldn't come up with a label he dared use in her presence.

"No, no boyfriend," she told the skipper in a voice that held no trace of regret. "My mother?" She glanced at him curiously. "What do you know about my mother?"

"Only what Asa Cox told me. That she was opposed to his hiring you. Said something about carving his heart out."

"That's my mother, all right. My father was lost at sea and . . . well, she's never gotten over it."

"A lot of men say that's the way they'd prefer to go."

Angie shook her head. "Not my father. He'd just be furious that the sea beat him."

"He was quite a man, your father."

"You knew him?"

"I sailed under him once. He wasn't the worst skipper I ever had." Abruptly the skipper straightened up, brushing his palms together briskly. "Anyway, the reason I was looking for you—we need coffee on the bridge. I don't want to have to keep reminding you about things like that. I'm not Long Jack, and this isn't your father's boat."

Angie stiffened. "Yes, sir." She turned on her heel, then stalked haughtily across the deck and through the walkway that led to the galley.

She could feel the skipper's narrow gray eyes following her, and the tiny hairs at the back of her neck prickled with something she chose to interpret as dislike.

So he had sailed with Cappy, she mused as she waited for the coffee to brew. Well, he hadn't learned much! She had begun this trip with a sneaking admiration for his blunt outspokenness; now she was beginning to believe it was nothing more or less than pure, unadulterated bad manners.

LIFE ABOARD the *Sea Witch,* Angie had to admit, was considerably different from her voyages aboard Cappy's old *Mackerel Sky.* Then, the crew had been like family. They had worked, played, married, lived and died together for generations. On a superseiner like this one, the crews were rearranged and reassigned every season. They had no shared history, no shared memories, no shared lives. It seemed to make the lonely necessity of being away from home nine months of the year even lonelier.

It certainly worked that way for Angie.

Dominic Oliphanta, deckboss on the *Sea Witch,* was the only member of the crew who had sailed with Long Jack in what he liked to call the "old days"—the days when the tuna trade was young and rough, and a man could still make his fortune with a line and a pole.

He was already a grandfather many times over when Angie shipped out for the first time on *Mackerel Sky,* and he had always treated her like one of his own large brood. Now his years showed plainly in his weathered face and grizzled gray hair. His body had thickened, and his back had acquired a stoop. Somewhere along the line, Angie noticed with a sense of outrage, he had grown old.

"It aint that the men dont like ye," he turned to explain to her one day, when he found her alone in the galley, floured to the elbows with the pie crust she was baking for the next day. "It's just that they gotta wait and see what yer made of. Long Jack's daughter ye may be, but yer a woman first. And a woman whose daddy and husband was lost at sea, well, it makes 'em nervous, dont ye know?"

Dominic often lingered in the galley after the crew had gone. He liked to reminisce, and he knew that Angie liked to listen. The other men, especially the young ones, interrupted his stories with anecdotes of their own, but Angie listened respectfully. That's what's missing in the younger generation, Dominic often thought gloomily—respect.

"Yeah," he continued, carefully filling his pipe from the pouch of Prince Albert he carried rolled up in the sleeve of his T-shirt. "Superstitious, they are. Well, hell, you know that. Even your daddy wore his weddin' ring slung on a gold chain around his neck. Know why he did that?"

Angie pushed her hair away from her forehead with the back of one floury hand and shook her head. Of course she knew—she had been raised on stories like these the way other kids were raised on fairy tales. But she also knew that Dominic relished the telling.

"Why, that's the price of admission to Davy Jones's locker, dont ye know! When a ship goes down, when all hope's lost, a man could let hisself go and feel like everything'd be all right."

He puffed furiously on the stem of pipe clenched between his teeth. "Yeah, most of the men'd feel foolish tryin' to explain it, but ye dont see many what aint got a bit of gold on 'em somewhere—a ring, or a gold tooth or maybe a gold plug in their ear.''

There were other superstitions. Angie knew them as well as Dominic. Beards, for example. They were often thought to be portends of a long trip, and there were still boats on which no man was allowed to grow one. On others, men had been known to shave a beard off with some unconvincing explanation when a trip had gone on too long.

Dominic was still ruminating. ''Yeah, used to wear a gold ring myself, but once it got caught in the net and took my finger clean off.'' He held up his left hand, where he had only three fingers and a thumb.

'''Course, I aint no fool.'' He chuckled shrewdly. ''Got a gold tooth now. Had a perfectly good one yanked out just so's I could get a gold one put in. Just foolishness, like I said, but . . . man dont take chances on a thing like that. Ye never know. No, sir, you just never know.''

He sucked meditatively on his pipe. ''Hell,'' he said after a moment. ''I bet even a skipper like this one, what got his papers right outta college, bet he's got a bit o' gold on 'im somewheres, too.''

With the prongs of a fork, Angie began trimming the circles of dough she had carefully draped over a row of battered aluminum pie tins. ''Not in a wedding ring, I notice,'' she offered, in what she hoped was a nonchalant manner.

''Noticed that, did ye?'' Dominic fixed his rheumy old eyes on her.

''Well, he *is* the skipper,'' she said defensively. ''Naturally I wonder about him.''

"Ye dont need to be wondering about him. Ye want to know something, ye ask old Dominic, eh? I'm like yer *pai,* yer father, ye know that, girl."

"I know that, Dominic."

"And I wouldn't feel square with yer daddy when I meet him again, may it be many years from now—" he crossed himself fervently "—if I didn't tell ye what ye ought to know."

"You know this skipper, then?" Angie tried to disguise the eagerness in her voice and failed entirely.

"I sailed with him before. And I'll tell you what I know. He's a good man. He can find fish. But Long Jack he aint." Dominic sat back in his chair with a disapproving sniff, as if he'd told her everything that mattered.

"But... what else? Does he have people? How long has he been with Montero's?"

"He's from up along San Pedro—what would I be knowin' about his people? Divorced, is what I hear."

Without quite knowing why, Angie felt relief flooding her face.

"That makes ye happy. Why? One woman left him, aint that enough for ye?" He reached across the table and patted her hand with one of his gnarled ones. "He aint the one for ye, girl. Long Jack'd be the first to tell you that. Ye listen to old Dominic, eh? Find yerself a feller, settle down, have babies, like ye oughtta done after Mano.

"And—" his voice fell lower "—just between ye 'n me, find yerself a doctor or a lawyer, someone what aint in the fleet, know what I mean?"

"Marry out of the fleet?" Angie pretended to be shocked. "You, of all people, tell me this?"

"I tell ye this," Dominic persisted. "I raised four daughters, and I say to ye what I said to them—a man what's gone nine months out of the year aint no kind of husband for a woman. Not for a lovin' woman."

Dominic had also raised five sons, all of whom were tuna fishermen; Angie wondered briefly at the paradoxical combination of love and tradition that made a man like Dominic encourage his sons to stay in the fleet, and his daughters to marry out of it.

"Well, you don't have to worry about me, Dominic," she said positively. "Marriage is the farthest thing from my mind."

"Oh? Then let me ask ye—how many *other* man jacks aboard this tub aint wearin' weddin' rings? Huh, didn't *think* ye'd know!"

With a weary sigh he slapped his palms flat on the table and pushed himself up from his chair. The pouches under his eyes sagged into the jowls of his leathery cheeks, and even the corners of his mustache drooped. "This old body," he grumbled, "it gets tired just *waitin'* for the fish."

He reached across the table and wiped a streak of flour from Angie's cheek with a fond, callused forefinger. "Ye listen to old Dominic, eh?" Then he hitched his pants over his girth and ambled out the hatch.

But there was something in Angie that couldn't heed Dominic's advice. This skipper was an enigma, a puzzle that aroused her curiosity despite her best attempts to ignore it.

He spent most evenings with his crew, playing cards around the long galley table and listening to their talk. Sometimes he contributed an anecdote or two, but Angie soon noticed that, mainly, he listened. There was always a cigarette dangling from the corner of his mouth, and often he was so still that the ash grew long at the tip.

But his passivity was misleading. His narrow eyes moved constantly, darting restlessly from one man's face to another. The cigarette in the corner of his mouth never betrayed the ceaseless activity of his eyes. What was he looking for? Angie wondered. What did he want?

Away from the galley, he ordered Angie around like a deck boy. Frequently he worked right through lunch, and then he would request that she run him up a tray. Only once had he ever done more than grunt a curt acknowledgement.

He'd swiveled around when she'd entered.

"You look tired, Reno," he'd said, steepling the tips of his fingers beneath his chin. His gleaming pewter eyes had the same intensity as when he studied the crew in the galley.

Beneath that scrutiny, Angie felt disarmed. She was trying to be a fisherman, but somehow, without her understanding quite how, he made her feel like a woman. And she wanted to regard him as The Skipper; but somehow, without her understanding that, either, she was always exquisitely aware of him as a man. It kept her decidedly off-balance.

"Is the job too much for you?" he said almost kindly. "I understand you've never worked on a boat this size before."

The dark smudges beneath her eyes answered Joseph's question the moment she walked in. She was living on a treadmill, and he knew it. The *Sea Witch* was three times the size of Reno's biggest boat, and any way you figured, that translated to triple the work. Not for the first time since she'd come aboard his boat, he doubted the wisdom of his decision to take her on.

But he couldn't regret it. She had been determined to ship out, he reminded himself. Better *Sea Witch* than some broken-down tub, which was the only kind of boat that would have been hiring so late in the season. And better me than ... *than what?*

His thoughts continued. Some other skipper, less scrupulous, maybe. After all, the only thing he, Joseph, was after was her fishery. Someone else might want...more. How long, jeered the caustic inner voice that was his conscience, was he going to be able to keep pretending it was only Reno Fisheries he wanted?

Standing before his desk, Angie squared her shoulders. Joseph tried not to notice how the movement thrust her full breasts forward. He tried not to notice the faint outline of nipples, suggesting that she wore only a T-shirt under her shirt. He tried not to notice the sudden, heavy ache in his groin.

"Has someone been complaining, sir?" she countered.

"Not at all." The chair squeaked as he fidgeted uncomfortably side to side. "But I thought that if you can't handle it, I might assign one of the men to give you a hand."

Angie smiled skeptically. "Tie an apron on one of those guys and they'd probably keel-haul me!"

With an involuntary smile, which he immediately suppressed, Joseph dismissed her. But later that evening Luis, the scrawny, surly fifteen-year-old who was serving a summer apprenticeship, appeared at the galley hatchway. "Skipper says I'm s'posed to see what you need done."

"You won't mind working in the galley?"

Luis shrugged. "Swabbin' decks, washin' dishes—it's all the same to me," he mumbled. "Either way I end up with dishpan hands."

ONLY ONE crew member was proving hard to deal with. His name was Saxby. Sax. If he had another, Angie didn't know it. He was the Number One speedboat driver, and he was, as were all the speedboat drivers, burly and powerful.

They *had* to be. When a school of fish was spotted, the small, flat-bottomed speedboats were immediately dropped overboard by the enormous crane. Their job was to herd the fish toward the tuna boat while it corralled the school in its net. The speedboats had to hit the water at full throttle, launched as they were from a vessel already traveling at thirty knots. If a driver's nerve failed for even a fraction of a second, he and his speedboat were lost.

Speedboat drivers were expected to be eccentric, and even admired for it. Sax, however, was a pirate even by speedboat driver parameters, and he sported a gold earring in one ear, just in case anyone should doubt it.

His eyes were close-set and angry above a nose that had been broken in just about every waterfront dive in the world. When he spoke, his voice was a vicious growl, and it seemed to Angie that his scurrilous language was deliberately and personally directed at her.

Why does Montero's keep him on? she wondered as she watched him snarl his way through meals. He wouldn't have lasted one season at Reno's. But this isn't Reno's, she reminded herself harshly. This is aquabusiness. This is the future. This—*bitterness* rose like bile in the back of her throat—is Montero's.

Chapter Five

Until the *Sea Witch* arrived at the fishing grounds, there wasn't much for the crew to do. So they played poker. Interminably.

The games went on for days, starting in the galley because it was the biggest space on the boat, moving to the fo'c'sle when the galley was in use, and then back to the galley again. The players were interchangeable, leaving the game to stand their watches while other men took their places.

Sometimes Angie watched, her feet wrapped around the rungs of a chair that was tipped back on two legs to lean against the bulkhead. She had witnessed this scene many times before—men in T-shirts and dungarees, sitting around a table playing poker in a blue haze of cigarette smoke—although the actors changed from year to year, boat to boat. Their arms were muscular, sometimes tattooed. They held their cards close to their chests, and snapped them down on the table with cool precision.

How wonderful, she sometimes thought, to be so free and so certain of everything—of women, and the sea and the next draw of the cards!

But there were other times when she felt as though she couldn't pretend to ignore one more ribald remark, or breathe in one more lungful of secondhand smoke.

Those times, feeling like the outsider the skipper had warned her she would be, she escaped with a book and a thermos of iced tea to a space she had discovered on the upper deck where no one else seemed to go.

One evening after supper when, paperback bestseller in hand, Angie climbed the ladder that led to the upper deck, she saw that her private space was already occupied.

It was Dominic, sitting against one of the speedboats. Propped between his legs was a giant tortoise shell, which he was rubbing energetically with a ragged chamois.

"Hi," she said. "Why aren't you down in the poker game?"

"Man gets tired of cards," Dominic grunted in greeting. "They got an old John Wayne movie on the VCR in the fo'c'sle, too, but a man gets tired of old movies 'n cheap novels, too. Sometimes a man's gotta do something with his hands."

"Oh?" Angie remarked caustically. "You mean like when I heard you guys out shooting sharks last night?"

Dominic had the grace to look sheepish. "We dont mean nothin' by it. It's somethin' to do, is all."

Angie let him off the hook. "That's going to be beautiful when you get it finished," she said, indicating the tortoise shell. "You don't see things like that much anymore."

"Well, it's somethin' to do." Dominic acknowledged, bending his head to his task. "Young fellas, they dont practice the old fishermen's arts like they used to." He shrugged. "Aint no big deal. Its just somethin'—"

"Something to do, yes, I know!" Angie sat down beside him and pulled her sunglasses out of her hair, settling them on her nose as she tilted her face toward the warmth of the sun. She stretched her legs in their denim cutoffs straight out on the deck and crossed them at the ankles.

"Haven't seen much of you lately," she commented after watching Dominic work for a while.

"Skipper keeps me pretty busy. It aint like it was on the old *Mackerel Sky,* big boat like this. Seems like there's allus somethin' needs doin'."

"Dominic," Angie began hesitantly, then took a deep breath and plunged ahead. "What made you decide to sign on with Montero's, anyway? My mother and I, we'd like to know. Weren't you happy with us?"

"It aint that, Angie girl...."

"What, then? I'm going to be running Reno's soon, and I'd like to know—what would it take to get you back?"

The old man looked uncomfortable. "Things're different in a big outfit like Montero's," he said slowly. "The men aint so close, not like it used to be when yer daddy was alive. But times change, ye know?" He sighed. "Now I just want to get my pension."

"You could fight, Dominic. The times don't have to change, not if people don't want them to...."

"*Sim,* yes. But me, I'm too old to fight. It's a job for younger men. And maybe the changes aint so bad, neither. If yer one of the man jacks what's jinxed to draw the short straw, maybe ye'd be glad fer a company what's got insurance. An' ye dont have to work 'til yer old bones wont hold ye up anymore—ye got yer pension.''

"I think you've sold your birthright for a pension," Angie said tartly. "That doesn't sound like you."

"I'm over sixty, girl. Ye get to be my age, ye start wonderin' how many more trips they're gonna let ye sign on for."

"Well, I just know Long Jack wouldn't have given in."

Dominic clucked his tongue in admiration. "Yer right about that! He was a fighter, was ol' Long Jack. Man'd go to hell 'n back for a skipper like that."

"And Long Jack was godfather to your first grandchild. This Montero skipper, what do you know about him? And what does he know about you? He—"

"He knows I had the biggest catch in the fleet, two years ago—"

Angie whirled her head around. On the ladder stood the skipper, only his head and big shoulders visible above the edge of the upper deck. She had no idea how long he'd been standing there. The man crept around on cat's-paws, she thought furiously!

"—And I know he's an excellent deckboss. He has a job with me for as long as he wants it." The skipper turned to Dominic. "They need you in the hold," he said, stepping aside to let Dominic pass. "Here, let me get that for you."

He reached out and Dominic passed him the shell. "I'll bring it by the fo'c'sle later. I'd like to have a closer look. I'm afraid I don't practice any of the fishermen's arts—I'm still into cheap novels and old movies."

As long as that! Angie was mortified.

"By the way," the skipper continued to Dominic, "fishing grounds tomorrow."

"Aye, sir! The men'll be happy t' hear it." Dominic disappeared down the ladder, his weathered old face wreathed in concentric circles of smiles.

"No, stay," the skipper said as Angie started to scramble to her feet. "I like to look at a pretty woman as well as the next man." He smiled. "Still inciting my crew to mutiny, I see."

"I *am* sorry, sir. I know it must seem that way to you. But . . . there are things I need to know, and this is the only way I can find them out."

"I could say 'not on my boat,' you know—and it would be quite within my rights to do so."

"I know," Angie said miserably.

He towered over her, the tortoise shell between his hands. She thought unexpectedly that he looked like nothing so much as a knight, straight and proud, and holding his shield before him. A *conquistador*, Charlotte would say.

"You're wrong, you know." He sat down opposite her, propping his elbows on his upraised knees, and Dominic's tortoise shell on the deck between his feet. "We—Montero's—care very much about the men who work for us. We have profit-sharing and a pension plan and medical insurance. We take better care of them than their union."

"Tunamen don't need anyone to take care of them. They can take care of themselves—they always have."

"And when something goes wrong, when a man doesn't come back, what happens to his people then?"

Angie's jaw set obstinately. "We've always looked out for our own," she insisted, although she was uncomfortably aware that the informal support system didn't always function as well as it should.

"Charity," he said distastefully. "What we do is make it possible for a man to develop his own long-range plans—so that he can retire someday, and so that his family will be provided for in case he doesn't make it that far. The form is different, maybe, but the function is the same."

He paused, eyeing Angie through inscrutable gray eyes. "You know, we're not really so far apart, you and I."

"You work for Montero's. We can't get any farther apart than that."

The skipper sighed. "You're a stubborn woman, Reno. I wonder if Long Jack ever taught you that there's a time to cut bait. That sometimes it's wiser to desert a sinking ship than to ride it clear to the bottom."

"I'm sure I don't know what you mean," Angie said with a haughty toss of her head.

"Think about it. It'll come to you, college girl like you." His words were vaguely belittling, although his expression remained bland and smiling.

She stirred uneasily. The deck seemed very warm beneath her.

"What's the matter, Reno?" the skipper inquired solicitously, cagily studying her face.

Involuntarily her eyes were drawn to the cleft in his chin that looked almost like a scar. The lips above it were dark and full, verifying a sensuality she had only suspected at a distance. The deck became suddenly much warmer.

"There's nothing the matter," she asserted.

His lips were so close that she could almost touch them with her own, if she wanted to—and she wondered abruptly if she did? Then a dark blush suffused her olive skin. What was the matter with her? He was the skipper, for God's sake, and a Montero man to boot!

The significance of the blush was not lost on the skipper. "It's hard being the only woman among twenty-four men, isn't it, Reno?" His voice was kind and circumspect, like a priest encouraging the confession of a reluctant penitent.

"Yes, it's hard," Angie replied faintly. "But you don't make it any easier."

"I don't *want* to make it any easier. I want to make it as difficult as possible." His voice was still very gentle. "I want to show you why women don't belong out here. The tuna trade's a rough business, lady—I don't think you've got the heart for it."

He leaned imperceptibly closer, and his words were low and suggestive. "Maybe you've forgotten what it's like to be a woman. Maybe you've forgotten what that lovely woman's body looks like—we only have those little shaving mirrors, and even those are all pitted. Maybe you've started to think you're just one of the guys around here. But you don't...*feel*...like one of the guys, do you?"

Angie knew she should disagree with everything he said, but a strange languor had overtaken her. It seemed to be composed in equal parts of the sun-warmed deck, the suggestive timbre of the skipper's voice and the dawning realization that he didn't think of her as "one of the guys."

Combined with the relaxing warmth of the sun, his voice was indeed hypnotic. It lulled her inhibitions like a siren's song.

Spellbound by the lips that were only inches away, she noticed with a compassionate pang the deep creases etched from his nose to his mouth. Carved there by years of exposure to the elements, they were incontrovertible proof of the harshness of the life he'd chosen.

She wanted to reach up and smooth away those hard lines with her fingertips, kiss them away with the softness of her own lips. Her eyelids fluttered half-closed, and her lips parted slightly, giving in to the abandon that was fast possessing the rest of her body.

"Is that why you don't wear a bra?" the skipper continued in the same calm, lulling voice. "You think nobody notices? Well, maybe nobody does. Maybe. But I wouldn't count on it!" A hearty chortle erupted from his lips, and his eyes danced wickedly.

The sudden gibe jolted Angie back to reality. She leapt to her feet and drew herself up to her full, considerable height. Her hands clenched furiously at her sides. "You speak to me that way again, Captain, and I'll have you up on charges! Sexual harassment for starts, and after that anything else I can think of!"

She glared at him with contemptuous eyes, enraged as much at herself as at him. What, after all, did she *expect* from a Montero man? The polished tortoise shell lay on the deck between his feet and hers like a fallen shield. *They aren't* conquistadors *anymore,* she heard Charlotte's distant, cynical voice reminding her.

"What harassment?" he asked innocently, squinting into the sun as he grinned at her wickedly. "I was only advising you on matters of dress. We don't want to have a morale problem on board this boat now, do

we? No, don't go." This was said as Angie turned on
her heel and prepared to descend the ladder. "I have to
get back to the bridge anyway."

He stood, tucked the shell securely beneath his arm
and disappeared down the ladder.

Angie sat back down on the sun-washed deck and
opened her book on her knees. I handled that well, she
congratulated herself. That's the last I'll hear from
Captain Callais! But she had to admit that he hadn't
looked the least bit chastened when he left, and she
wondered suddenly if she had handled it all that well,
after all.

A picture of long, denim-clad legs scissored across
her mind, closely followed by other, even more dis-
turbing images. The humid air was suddenly stifling.
Angie piled her tousled hair on top of her head and
held it there with both hands, exposing her perspiring
nape to the hope of a breeze.

Unable to concentrate on the printed pages before
her, she closed the book and focused her attention instead on the horizon. Lines of white clouds scudded
across the sky, trailing pink and orange ribbons in the
wake of the setting sun.

Descended from generations of seafarers on both
sides of her family, Angie read the sky without even
realizing that she did so. It was instinct to a people
whose survival until very recently had depended on
how well they interpreted the sky.

Red sky at night, sailor's delight. She saw that they
would arrive at the fishing grounds on a good day.

Chapter Six

"Who goes there?" challenged the watch. "Oh, it's you, Reno. Can't sleep, eh? Aint surprised—big day tomorra." He motioned her on with the beam of his flashlight.

Angie walked to the foredeck. As she rounded the bridge, she saw the red tip of a cigarette glowing in the dark. *Everyone must be restless tonight,* she thought, deciding to look elsewhere for a little privacy.

"Reno." Joseph's voice spoke out of the darkness. The tip of his cigarette bobbed.

Angie joined him at the rail. "How'd you know it was me?"

"I've been watching the light in the galley go on and off for the last half hour." The moonlight gentled his rough-hewn profile, making him attractive in a much more conventional way. "I was hoping you'd come up here."

"Oh? Why?"

"Well, for one thing, I thought you'd enjoy the whales."

"Whales?"

"Sure. Look, over there. You can see them plain as day when the moon's full." He put his arm around her shoulder and turned her in the direction his other hand was pointing. "Do you see them?"

"Yes. Yes, I do!" She watched in delight as several dark, glistening humps dove in and out of the moonlit waves.

"These are the last of the summer migration down from the Arctic. Young adults—must have gotten off to a late start." Two whales surfaced together, one showing its huge head, the other its enormous flukes. "Those must be the males," Joseph said. "See that hump to the right? That's probably the female. This is their courtship routine."

"And she'll pick one?"

"Or both. Or more. Whale propagation gets incredibly complicated."

The *Sea Witch* glided almost noiselessly through the placid seas, following a path of moonlight that shimmered all the way to the horizon. Flying fish flashed with silvery iridescence as they leapt over the bow.

"I'd forgotten how beautiful the sea can be at night," Angie said wistfully.

When the whales had gone deep, signaling their departure with blows that looked like waterspouts, Joseph's arm remained around Angie's shoulders, quite as though he'd forgotten it altogether.

After the scene they'd had on the bridge earlier that evening, Angie was surprised that she felt so comfortable with him. Everybody was tense, she reminded herself. Probably he hadn't meant the remarks he made earlier to be rude and tactless. Probably he *had* only been advising her on matters of dress. Probably she had overreacted.

Unconsciously she relaxed into the curve of his arm, and felt it tighten around her. She was exquisitely aware of the pressure of his forearm across her shoulders, the solid muscle flexed behind her neck, the idle brush of his fingers back and forth across her upper arm.

Has it been hard for him, she wondered, the life of a fisherman? The living between two worlds, never truly at home in either? It could be exciting, and it could be romantic, but what it essentially was, was lonely.

Angie's glance left the shimmering path of moonlit water and fell closer, to where her hand and his rested side by side on the brass rail. She felt an almost irresistible urge to slip her own hand under his broad, brown one, to rest her head in the inviting hollow of his shoulder. Just for a little while. Just for tonight. Vague yearnings welled up inside her, yearnings that she hadn't felt for a long time and barely recognized now. They had a piercing sweetness.

"Tell me about yourself," Joseph suggested. His breath moved softly against her temple; Angie could almost imagine it was a kiss.

"What would you like to know?"

"Tell me about your husband. You loved him very much?"

"Yes. But we were so young. Sometimes I can't believe I was ever that young." She sighed—a poignant sound that resembled a sob, but with all the emotion long since drained away—as she remembered the youthful, exuberant way Mano had loved her. It seemed like a very long time ago.

"Do you still miss him?"

"Not exactly. I tried not to forget—I felt I owed him that much. But it was no use. He's been gone longer now than I knew him. I can *remember* what I felt, but

I can't *feel* that way anymore. I guess now I just miss...having love in my life."

Then she gave a shaky laugh. "I never said that before. I didn't even know I thought it. It makes me feel so...disloyal."

"Your first loyalty is to yourself, Reno. It was a terrible tragedy, but you're still alive, and you've got your own life to live." He paused. "You haven't married again. Why?"

"That's what everyone expected me to do," Angie said, more than a little astonished at her own frankness. "I expected it myself. It was all I'd ever planned to be—a wife, a mother someday. But I found..."

"What?"

"That there wasn't a man I knew that I couldn't squash ten of." Instantly she regretted her candor, but Joseph only chuckled.

"I can believe that!" he said emphatically, and Angie thought she detected a hint of relish in his voice. "So...what? That's when you decided to go to college?"

"It was my mother's idea, actually. She saw me floundering." *We've washed up on some pretty rocky shoals, baby. As I see it, we can let the tide break us up on the rocks, or we can let it float us free. It's up to us now.*

"She suggested I enroll in some business courses and learn what I needed to know to take over Reno's, and she would keep it running until I graduated. It brought some purpose to her life, too, I guess. I don't think she wanted to go on after my father died. They had a very—" she paused delicately, searching for the right word "—*passionate*...relationship. I think she finds life...empty...without him."

Joseph nodded in the dark. "It takes special people to maintain that kind of marriage, especially when the man is gone to sea nine months out of the year."

"What it takes is a woman who's able to overlook a whole lot of things. My mother was that kind of woman."

She knew that for some tunamen, the long separations were a drawback to life in the fleet, while for others, it was one of the advantages. She suspected which it had been with Cappy, a smile always on his face and money always in his pocket. But she also knew, as her mother did, that whichever it had been, it had nothing to do with the love he bore for Charlotte.

"And what does it take from the man?"

"Well, I'm not sure," Angie replied in the same frank way. "But I think it must take a man who's...worth it."

Joseph took a deep drag on his cigarette and then flicked it overboard. "What about your husband?" he said after a moment. "Was he worth it?"

Mano flashed across her mind, not the shadowy figure he had become in her memory, but for a moment virile and vital and alive. She saw him, his navy blue pea coat slung over one shoulder, strutting in his happy-go-lucky way up the stairs to their tiny apartment with all the cocky gaiety of a sailor home on shore leave. "He would have been, I think."

"How about the men you met in college? I can't imagine how they let you get away."

"College boys!" she scoffed. The contempt in her voice said more than her words. "Actually, they weren't all that interested."

With a slight twist of his body Joseph turned toward her. The subtle shift surprised Angie, and she looked questioningly at him. His suddenly smoldering eyes shone like burnished pewter in the moonlight.

"There isn't a man in the world who wouldn't be interested in you," he said gruffly. His forearm tightened behind her neck.

He was going to kiss her. She knew it. And she knew beyond a shadow of a doubt what her response was going to be. Her glance flickered down to his lips as they moved toward hers in the moonlight.

"And, besides," she continued, "there was always...Reno's...." Her voice trailed off and finally stopped altogether.

The movement of his lips died stillborn. "Ah, yes. Reno's." Slowly and deliberately he released her, letting his arm fall from behind her neck. He turned back to the rail. "Thanks for reminding me," he said after a moment.

"Of what?" she asked, bewildered.

"Of priorities. Yours. And mine." He pulled another cigarette from his pocket and lit it with an unsteady hand.

"I'm sorry," he added after a moment. "There are some who would call this 'sexual harassment.'"

Angie flushed, recalling the threat she'd made that afternoon on the speedboat deck. "I was angry."

"You were right."

She studied his profile unhappily. Backlighted by the moon, it looked stern and unyielding. *Priorities?* What on earth did he mean by that? Now that the moment had passed, Angie was mortified by her instinctive response to a man who was really no more than a stranger to her.

The silence lengthened awkwardly.

"Well, maybe I'd better go below," she offered.

Joseph didn't turn his gaze away from the horizon. His elbows were propped on the rail, and the glowing tip of his cigarette was suspended between two fingers over the water.

When he gave no indication that he had heard, Angie turned and walked back to the galley.

EVEN AFTER SHE HAD returned to bed, sleep eluded her. Her tiny, windowless cabin, nothing more than a converted storeroom, really, was stifling. Beads of sweat formed between her breasts and tickled as they trickled downward. Her body felt leaden and unfamiliar as she tossed restlessly from side to side.

Later, she heard footsteps above her head. Joseph had returned to his quarters. But not to sleep. After a while she heard footsteps. Back and forth, back and forth. Pacing.

Chapter Seven

Before full light, Joseph came into the galley.

Unaffected by his long night of pacing, a sort of nervous energy possessed him. He moved restlessly around the galley floor on the balls of his feet, like a prizefighter spoiling to get into the ring.

He was unable to sit still even long enough to eat. He wolfed his fried eggs, *chorizo*—the turtle-meat sausage that was a favorite with tunamen—toast and coffee while standing at the porthole, observing the large number of fishing vessels that now surrounded them.

"Ever seen anything so beautiful in your life?" he demanded proudly of Angie.

She smiled. He had every right to be pleased with himself. The presence of so many other boats in the area confirmed that in the relentless roulette the skippers played with each other, he had proven himself savvy. It was a skill—an instinct, really, this ability to eavesdrop on coded high-seas radio transmissions between rival boats, and correctly decipher them to find out where in the vast fishing grounds fish were being caught.

After reminding Angie to send a pot of coffee up the halyard about ten o'clock, Joseph headed out the hatch. By the time the crew began to straggle in for breakfast, he was already up the mast and on the glasses, searching for fish.

Angie could tell that the men, in their taciturn way, were as excited as Joseph. While she cooked each individual breakfast to order, flipping pancakes for one, frying *chorizo* and eggs for another, serving Dominic the sweet rolls she knew he shouldn't have, she listened to their fragmentary conversation.

"My uncle knew a guy sailed under the skipper once, couple'a years back," one fisherman volunteered. "Said he knows his stuff."

Silence fell while the men concentrated on their food.

"I never signed on a company boat before," commented another. "When it ain't family, you don't know what to expect."

"Hell." The first man shrugged. "I never did any better with my father-in-law than I did with anyone else."

"There's skippers and there's skippers," grunted one of the brawny speedboat drivers. "Heard this one got record hauls, few years back. He'll do all right by us."

"No way, man!" someone snorted. "He's from up along San Pedro! What do those guys know about running a boat?"

"Must know something," the driver countered laconically. "They're taking over the whole damn fleet. Pretty soon, won't be anyone left in San Diego. Then it won't make no nevermind what you think—you wanna work, you go up along. Or to Taiwan. Any of you guys ready to learn Chinese?"

"Hell, I got enough trouble with you Port-a-gee!" drawled a young blond giant nicknamed Tennessee, although that was neither his birthplace nor his name.

It was simply because he spoke with a Southern twang as slow and thick as molasses.

"The skipper, he's all right," the speedboat driver said again. "He'll put us on fish."

Sax, who had been silent while the sneer on his face deepened, slapped his hands on the table. "You bastids don't know yer arse from first base," he jeered. "He works for Montero—they sent him down to Dago. That's gotta tell ye something! He's trouble, that's what it tells me!

"They don't want him up there, prob'ly no one'll sign on with him, that's what *I* say! Look'a here, he takes on this broad—what for? I wasn't born yestiddy, even if ye bastids was! *I* know why he's got her aboard! And I'll tell you another thing—there aint no trusting a skipper what's leading with his crotch!"

He pushed himself up from the table with his massive forearms, shoving his heavy chair backward. It hit the bulkhead with a dull thud. Before Angie could move out of the way, he had flung himself past her, slamming her into the cookstove as he snarled a malevolent oath and stomped out the hatch.

An embarrassed silence fell around the table. The other speedboat driver aimed a disgusted look in the direction Sax had disappeared, then stood and followed him out. "'Scuse me, ma'am," he said to Angie as he edged around her with a gesture that would have been a tip of his hat if he'd been wearing one.

"C'mon, Reno," another one said gruffly. "Don't pay no nevermind to Sax. He's just nervous, is all. He gits on fish, he'll be all right. Sit yourself down here and have a cup o'joe." He righted the chair Sax had overturned and, with a brusque jerk of his head, beckoned Angie to sit.

She poured herself a cup of coffee and slid into the place vacated by Sax. His plate with its half-eaten food felt dirty as she pushed it out of her way. The chair felt dirty. Even the air he had occupied felt dirty.

I should have defended myself, she seethed, drinking the coffee in huge gulps that burned her mouth. *I should have done something!*

But she had been to sea often enough to know that aboard a boat, where the men's very lives depended on each other, direct confrontations were always avoided. The most ominous threat Angie had ever heard one man issue to another was "Wait 'til we get back to Dago!"—and even that had been forgotten when the boat rounded the tip of Point Loma on its homeward journey.

After giving the matter some thought, she decided that the best course would be to keep as much distance as possible between herself and Sax. She was, after all, an interloper in this world, as Joseph had pointed out.

One by one the fishermen filed out of the galley, most of them going topside to line up at the rail and estimate the chances of an early set. Angie was left alone at the silent table, feeling even more isolated than usual.

What had she expected from this trip? she wondered, as she scraped the plates desultorily and submerged them in soapy water. There was no time for philosophy, no time to ponder the mysteries of the sea. There was barely time enough to *think* in the dreary, never-ending round of producing three meals a day for twenty-four men.

The food aboard the tuna boats was legendary—it was one of the compensations for being away from home nine months of the year. A good cook understood that; and a *great* cook could command a salary even higher than the skipper's. And Angie had determined when she signed on that she would be a *great* cook, at least for the duration. A Reno could do no less.

Breakfasts were always cooked to order; beside the usual offerings of eggs, pancakes, and toast, there was also more exotic fare—turtle meat, *huevos rancheros* and freshly made doughnuts and sweet rolls. Lunch and dinner were always full-course meals, beginning with appetizers and cocktails, and finishing with fancy, homemade desserts.

She outdid herself. Even the men who'd had grave doubts about the wisdom of sailing with a woman came to appreciate the spectacular meals she served.

But there was a price, and Angie paid it every night when she stumbled into her tiny bunk. She was asleep before her head hit the pillow, and she slept as if drugged, until the nightwatch banged on the galley door at four o'clock in the morning to wake her to another day of drudgery.

Sullen, undersize Luis helped with the scut work, of course, when she could pin him down. But much of the time he drifted out of the galley with the rest of the men, and Angie couldn't blame him. She would have done the same thing, if she'd had half a chance!

What was it about this life that fascinated some men so? What made them go out year after year, in spite of the hardship, in spite of the danger?

It paid exceptionally well, of course, but there were other jobs, safer jobs, ashore that paid equally well. Nevertheless, once a man had been a fisherman for a few years, he almost never left the fleet. It got into his blood, somehow.

Like this skipper, this Joseph Callais. Young, educated. He could do anything he chose to do with his life. And yet there he was, perched thirty-eight feet in the air, baking under the merciless sun, scanning the trackless sea through binoculars for signs of fish.

After a few hours in the crow's nest he would be sweltering. And if he was anything like Cappy, he'd probably be impetuous enough to strip off his long-sleeved work shirt, so that by the time he came down, he would be miserably sunburned. It always happened early in the season; by September, his skin would have built up layer upon layer of sunburn until it was as impervious as a shell.

Angie discovered that she couldn't think of Joseph's sunburned arms without thinking of the way one of them had felt, draped across her shoulders last night. Possessively, almost as though it was his right.

His boat. *His* crew. *His* world. A man like that could take what he wanted—who would deny him? He could have kissed her last night, and she would have been helpless in his arms. He probably could have done a great deal more than that if he chose, she suspected, and she would have been just as helpless to resist.

A stab of desire, as piercing and as sweet as the one that had assailed her last night, coursed through her body again. Just for a moment she allowed herself to imagine what it would be like to *belong* to a man like that, in all the thrilling, secret ways a woman can belong to a man. To be the woman a man like that came home to...

Sponge in one hand, she took a last soapy swipe at the plate she held in the other, then transferred it to the next sink to be rinsed.

IT WAS LONG past suppertime, and only Dominic still sat at the table. His eyes were at half-mast, and a coffee cup teetered precariously in his hand. When Joseph came through the hatch, Dominic looked up and saw something in his expression that made the old man mumble good-night, then creak to his feet and shuffle out.

Joseph wore only gray sweatpants with a drawstring waist that rode low on his hips, and a white towel draped around his neck. Fine, dark hair formed a thick mat on his chest, and his skin was tanned—except for his face, neck and arms, which were a fiery red. His hair was damp and he smelled of soap, with the hint of Old Spice that almost but not quite concealed the pervasive shipboard odor of diesel fuel.

He seemed uncomfortable, and apparently not due entirely to the sunburn that looked very painful indeed. His eyes darted all around the room, meeting Angie's only briefly before shifting away again. Thrusting his hands into the pockets of his sweats, he slouched on one hip and addressed the floor.

"Look..." he began, then cleared his throat and tried again. "I feel I should apologize for last night." His voice was very stiff and formal. "I was...not myself. I should not have taken advantage of your position. I am, after all, the skipper."

That out of the way, he visibly relaxed. Sitting down at the head of the table, he leaned back in the chair and propped his elbows on the arms. He crossed his legs so that the ankle of one rested on the knee of the other, gave Angie a boyish grin, and said, "Coffee?"

The baggy sweats and the towel did little to conceal the impressive physique they covered. Of course all the men dressed in the same scant way in the warm climates, but Angie could honestly say that she had never considered it anything more than a matter of comfort and convenience. Until now.

She poured the reheated coffee into a chipped white mug. Black, the way he took it. Then she got a bowl and a clean cloth from one cupboard and a bottle of vinegar from another, and placed them on the table in front of him.

"What's that?" he asked warily, looking first at the bowl and then up at Angie.

Instead of replying, she partially filled the bowl with vinegar and dipped the cloth into it. Then, sitting on the chair catercorner from him, she proceeded to apply the pungent liquid to one sunburned arm.

Joseph looked embarrassed. "Hey, you don't have to do that," he protested.

"Of course I don't," she retorted, dipping the cloth again and patting it over his other arm. "But it always took care of my father's sunburn." She continued to wipe the damp cloth over his arms, then rose and walked behind his chair to gently dab it along the back of his neck.

His shoulders rippled as he moved his head right to left and back again, luxuriating in the soothing sting of the vinegar. "I heard you had some trouble with Sax today."

"I wish you hadn't." Angie dipped the cloth again and pressed it to his neck. "I handled it. It won't happen again, I'm sure."

Slowly, almost sensuously, she moved the damp cloth across his skin. She found herself wishing he had taken his shirt off up in the crow's nest so that she might have had a reason to stroke the vinegar down the long, muscled curve of his back. The towel covered his shoulders, and Angie lifted it out of the way as she daubed the vinegar lower. She tried to ignore the illogical but strangely compelling notion that she was undressing him.

"I wish I could be as sure as you are about it," he rumbled. "Believe me, Reno, if I'd known more about Sax before this trip started, I wouldn't have subjected you to this. He's a rough character, but he's the best speedboat driver in the fleet. Fearless. And you know what that can mean to a boat."

She knew. It was hands-down the most dangerous job in a fishing process fraught from beginning to end with danger. "I can handle Sax," she repeated with conviction. "Don't worry about me."

"Of course I worry about you. You're one of my crew, and I won't have a member of my crew abused. You know, Reno—" he cocked his head to look up at her "—I had a number of reasons for taking you on. Maybe not such good reasons, but I thought they were, at the time."

"I had reasons of my own, Skipper," Angie replied, meeting his eyes with a smile. "I thought they were good at the time, and I still do. It was a fair trade." Calmly she dipped the cloth again and pressed it against his neck.

"I know your reasons. I understand them. Asa Cox told me some of it—the rest of it I guessed."

He smiled ironically as her eyes widened. "Why does that surprise you? The kind of life we lead—it gets harder and harder to say what we feel. Sometimes we even stop trying—but that doesn't mean we stop feeling."

He looked up as Angie circled around in front of him and began patting the cloth over the angular planes of his face. "Outsiders don't see that. They don't see what's inside—they think that what they see is all there is. Sometimes even our own people can't see it. My wife didn't."

Reaching up, he closed his fingers around her wrist, bringing her hand to a halt midair. "You knew I was married?"

She nodded. "Dominic told me."

"Did he also tell you I'm divorced?" He released her wrist and looked down again while she continued to smooth his forehead with the soft cloth. "Everyone has a story, I guess. Mine's no different from a thousand others. She just got tired of being alone. One day I came home and she wasn't. That's all."

"I'm sorry."

He shrugged. "Don't be. It was a long time ago. Anyway, Reno, I'm sorry, too. Sorry I got you into this." He lifted his coffee mug to his lips and drained it. "I never meant you to be hurt."

"Hurt?" she repeated, her dark brows knit together in confusion. "Is this about Sax? There's nothing he can dish out that I can't handle—"

"No!" he roared suddenly. He struck the table with one clenched fist. The coffee mug rattled and the vinegar sloshed in the bowl. "No! This has nothing to do with Sax! It has to do with *me!*"

He pounded the table again, and glowered at Angie. The anger in his eyes seemed to suggest that she was somehow responsible for it. Then, dropping his eyes abashedly, he stood and crossed the galley to stand with legs widespread in front of the porthole.

The porthole was a glazed black circle that duplicated everything behind it as faithfully as a mirror, and because his back was to the room, Angie saw Joseph's

scowling face reflected back at her. He gripped the
dangling ends of the towel in his hands and jerked it
more firmly around his neck. She saw him wince as the
rough terry cloth scraped his sunburned skin.

"It's only this," he growled, his eyes seeking hers in
the salt-encrusted glass. "I won't have a member of my
crew abused—by *anyone*. Not by Sax, and certainly not
by me!"

He unlatched the metal frame of the porthole and
swung it outward, banishing the reflection of the galley and replacing it with the night sky and a million
brilliant stars. A warm tropical breeze wafted in. "You
don't know anything about me," he said strangely.

Angie smiled from where she stood at the table, the
damp cloth still clutched in her hand. "You're a good
skipper. What else do I need to know? 'An honorable
man,' Dominic said. You can find fish that got no tails
is the way he put it, and that's the ultimate compliment as far as he's concerned."

Joseph turned around and leaned backward against
the counter. "I'm not interested in what Dominic
thinks of me," he said brusquely.

"Well, not just Dominic... I mean, the whole crew,
everyone... respects you...."

He made a single, harsh sound that started out as a
laugh, but ended up sounding suspiciously like a groan.
"No, Reno. It isn't respect we're talking about here."
He pinned her with a gaze that made her feel like a
butterfly under a microscope. "I know what I felt last
night, and it had nothing to do with honor. Or respect.

"No, don't fidget like that." This last was said as
Angie lowered her eyes and the wet cloth, not sure what
to do with either one of them. "Don't you think I know

I could have kissed you last night? And it wasn't *honor*—'' he spat the word out as if it were bitter on his tongue ''—that stopped me. If Madruga hadn't been on the bridge... You wanted it, too. Don't you think I could tell?''

He smiled. It was only a cynical twisting of his lips. ''Don't look so shocked. I said we were *inarticulate*, Reno—I didn't say we were *insensitive.*''

Remembering last night embarrassed Angie, but even more urgently than that, it made her want to feel his arms around her again, feel him bending over her mouth as if he wanted to devour it. ''It was... a mistake.'' She faltered. ''It must have been—the whales—''

Over the lingering odors from supper, the night breeze through the porthole carried the tangy smell of vinegar and soap across the room. Angie's body swayed toward the source of the scent. He sensed her vulnerability and the hard muscles of his midsection tightened in desperate self-discipline.

''It was a mistake,'' he agreed, the cynical smile deepening. ''But it wasn't the whales.''

He released the ends of the towel and thrust his hands instead into the pockets of his sweats, settling the drawstring waistband dangerously lower on his hips. ''You know, I even considered leaving you behind, that first day you came on board. And I would have, if there'd been any way I could have gotten another cook on such short notice. I just... Well, I wanted you to know that.''

There seemed to be something more he wanted to say, but instead he turned and reached out the porthole, pulling it closed and snapping the latch.

"I'd better not keep you up any longer, Reno," he said. "Thanks for the first aid."

He flashed her a perfunctory "skipper" smile and, before she had a chance to reply, was gone. Immediately she heard footsteps running quickly up the ladder to the speedboat deck, then as quickly to his quarters behind the bridge.

Chapter Eight

Hundreds of sleek, glistening dolphins frolicked playfully through the open sea, breaking the surface of the water in unison like a well-trained drill team.

They "carried" the tuna, the fishermen liked to say. The two schools traveled together, the oxygen-breathing porpoises cavorting near the surface and giving evidence of the tuna that swam beneath them in the deeper, colder depths.

It was Madruga who spotted them first.

The rumored sighting crackled over the intercom. It summoned the fishermen away from the poker game, up from the engine room and out of the fo'c'sle.

It brought Angie topside, too, where she slouched against the rail of the speedboat deck, watching the fishing process swing into action around her. Until the fish were stored safely in wells deep in the bowels of the boat, she knew she was off duty. The men would work around-the-clock, eighteen or twenty-four hours at a stretch, and meals would be skipped altogether.

Madruga came down the mast, and Joseph climbed up. From the vantage point of the crow's nest, he ordered the speedboats dropped over the side while the school of yellowfin tuna was still six miles away.

Sax was in Number One, the only speedboat in radio contact with the skipper, while Pinheiro, Velasques, Riley and Tennessee zigzagged their own small boats in his wake.

The tiny crafts slammed against the water just long enough for their propellers to thrust them out again, airborne for several thrilling seconds between each thrust. They flew from the crest of one wave to the crest of the next, following Number One with blind faith as Sax searched for routes of passage through the trackless sea.

Sax was good, Angie had to admit, watching the speedboats disappear in the distance. He was very, very good. His performance was quite simply the best display of speedboat driving she'd ever seen. She could just about forgive him his repellent personality when she saw him operate his boat with all the grace of a ballet dancer, and the speed of a runaway train.

Joseph, still up the mast, ordered the launching of the skiff. The lumbering, flat-bottomed barge slid off the stern amidst a flurry of flying cable and rattling chains.

The skiff driver was a Portuguese named Lucas, nicknamed Show Biz for some long-forgotten exploit on some long-forgotten boat. His engine coughed to life, then began to tow the *Sea Witch,* now dead in the water, in a gigantic circle while the seiner fed the net off her stern.

The *Sea Witch* spread her entire seven tons of net, completely surrounding the school of yellowfin. Then the skiff towed her back to the point where the set had begun, closing the circle and capturing the fish in a mile-wide corral of net.

Joseph ordered the powerful boom into action.

It hauled the net out of the water and high into the air. The net tightened like a drawstring and concentrated the dense catch even further.

On a smaller vessel, the cook would have participated in the fishing process; here, Angie was only a spectator. But even as a spectator, she found herself vicariously sharing the adventure.

It was both terrifying and exciting. She heard herself shouting encouragement to the crew, automatically slipping into the vernacular she had grown up with—the slurred pidgin of English, Portuguese, Spanish and Italian that the fishermen used to communicate with each other.

Hoisted high overhead, the net fed steadily through the boom. Soon the tuna were as compact as bricks in a wall. Then the men began to unload the fish, tossing them onto conveyer belts that carried them to the hold.

All sorts of flotsam came up with the net and rained on the men working below. Angie blanched when an enormous jellyfish rode up entangled in the net, where it was shredded by the boom and dropped back down on the men like stinging nettles. The poisonous fragments slid agonizingly under their collars, into their gloves and through the most microscopic rents and tears in their protective clothing.

Jellyfish were painful, but they weren't the worst of the things that rode up in the net.

Upon hearing the cry *Ojos arriba!*—eyes up!—Angie saw Dominic glance upward, then nonchalantly step aside as a three-hundred-pound shark shook free of the net and fell sixty feet to the deck below. Although the shark grazed his shoulder, Dominic didn't even give the carcass a second look, nor did he lose a beat in the hoarse stream of invectives he was unleashing on the men.

And then there were the dolphins. To the superstitious fishermen they were thought to be good luck—they carried the tuna, didn't they?—and the crew worked hard to ensure that dolphins didn't perish unnecessarily. When one became entangled along with the deeper-swimming tuna, someone had to go into the net to release it.

The task required more dexterity than strength, and aboard the *Mackerel Sky,* it had been one of Angie's favorite duties. Impulsively she jumped to her feet and ran to her quarters, returning with a hard hat and a pair of boots she scavanged from the corner of a dusty storeroom.

The mood on deck was frenzied. Over the earsplitting grind of the boom, the men shouted to each other in their colorful pidgin, interspersed with loud Anglo-Saxon words whose meanings were unmistakable.

The brailing—the unloading of the catch—was being carried out under Dominic's eagle eye. Angie picked her way around the heaps of net and fallen sharks to where he stood. She grinned impishly. She wouldn't have expected this grandfatherly man to even *know* the kind of words that were spewing like a blasphemous litany from his mouth!

He glanced quickly over his shoulder. "Get back!" he shouted furiously, elbowing her roughly aside.

"I want to work!"

He hesitated; then, possibly remembering another set on another boat, he jerked his head in the direction of the net. "Go fer it!" he yelled gruffly.

Gripping the thick skeins of rope with both hands, Angie waded into the open mouth of the net. She moved slowly and cautiously in the dim half-light. Hand over hand she felt her way along the net, following shouted directions from the men outside as they voice-guided her toward a trapped dolphin. The huge tuna made a trembling floor beneath her feet.

As she stumbled across the writhing backs of the fish, she felt an occasional scrape of fins or teeth even through her protective clothing. The tuna didn't actually bite, she reminded herself nervously, but a two-hundred-pound fish has a big mouth and very sharp teeth—she had never gotten out of the net without a few scratches and abrasions, and it appeared that this time would prove no exception.

The thrashing of the fish and the grind of the brailer were muffled by the water, so that the undersea world surrounding her was strangely hushed. Voices drifted toward her from outside, but they were also muffled, the words vague and indistinguishable, the meanings lost.

Time seemed to slow and then to stop. Angie stopped, too, trying to understand the words that were almost unintelligible but at the same time, eerily familiar. How many times had these voices—no, not *these* voices, she amended confusedly, but others like them—guided her stumbling progress through this alien, twilight world?

With fingers hooked around the thick skeins of rope, Angie struggled to maintain her balance, her feet in their bulky seaboots trying to brace themselves on a rolling foundation as insubstantial as the voices themselves.

The years fell away. Suddenly she was sixteen again. The voices on deck belonged to Dominic, a much younger Dominic, and to Long Jack. How absurd, she thought for one brief, illogical moment, that she had imagined Dominic was old, and Cappy was...

Oh, Cappy, I had the most awful dream, she would tell him when she climbed out of the net, and Cappy would hug her close and laugh at her fears and make them all disappear....

"Reno!" A strident voice shattered the muffled silence. It jerked her harshly back to reality. She turned in confusion toward the source of the sound and saw several blurred, disembodied heads silhouetted in the daylight at the mouth of the net.

"Reno!" the voice bellowed again.

She reached down quickly and released the frantic dolphin, which streaked away in a wake of luminescent bubbles. Then she clambered over the slippery mass of tuna, and made her way back toward the voices and the light.

The cold water numbed her, and she and everything around her seemed to be moving in slow motion.

Looking up again, she saw the same ring of indistinguishable faces peering at her. For a wild, lightheaded instant she didn't know who would be waiting when she emerged from the net. Cappy, his arms opened wide to sweep her up in a jovial bear hug, or—? She reached for the daylight and staggered onto the deck.

Rough hands gripped her and hauled her to her feet. They stood her up none-too-gently on the deck.

"What do you think you're doing?" The rough hands belonged to the skipper, as did the bellowing voice. Elbows akimbo, he glowered nose-to-nose over Angie like a drill sergeant, forcing her to fall back a few steps from his outraged tongue-lashing. *"Just what in the hell do you think you're doing?"*

She swayed for a disoriented instant, suspended somewhere between the past and the present, and the skipper roughly seized her arm and shook her like a rag doll. Her dark eyes stared blankly into his seething gray ones. Then slowly her heart plummeted to the pit of her stomach and she realized, finally, incontrovertibly, that it had been no bad dream. Dominic was indeed old. Cappy was dead. And there was no jovial hug—just this raging bull of a skipper chewing her out in full view of the entire crew as if she were the greenest of greenhorns!

"Are you trying to get yourself killed?" the skipper snarled. His fingers dug like steel into her flesh. He gave her one last, punishing shake, then released her.

"I'll see you on the bridge, Reno," he snapped. "On the double!" Moving clumsily in his rubber boots, he turned and stalked away.

The brailing surged on around Angie as her eyes focused unhappily on the skipper's retreating back. The rapport she had felt with him the night before drained out of her, and once again he had become an unknown entity. She shot Dominic an apologetic look, then turned and followed in the skipper's footsteps.

Hurriedly she detoured into her cabin, where she threw her hard hat onto her bunk. Looking in the tiny shaving mirror on the wall she saw that her hair was a disheveled mop. She gave it a few quick licks with her hairbrush, succeeding only in creating a damp, frizzled bush.

Suddenly the breath caught painfully in her throat. In the cloudy mirror her startled eyes glimpsed the blurred reflection of someone standing directly behind her—a smear of sunburned flesh and the darker, redder smudge of a sweat-stained muscle shirt.

She whirled around. "Sax!" she exclaimed. He was standing in the doorway, staring into her cabin with his dull, angry eyes. "What are you doing here?"

He didn't answer. Nor did he move. He continued to block the door, staring unblinkingly at her in the way he had that made her feel somehow... dirty.

With an aplomb she was far from feeling, Angie lifted her chin. "Something I can do for you, Sax?" she asked.

"Food," Sax grunted, his thick, loose lips barely moving.

"Sure," Angie said. She relaxed, ashamed of her first, instinctive reaction. Her smile became a little friendlier. Sax had done a magnificent job out there, she thought. He had every right to be hungry! "There're sandwiches in the reefer, and there's a pot of *caldo verde* on the back burner. Just help yourself."

She moved as if to head out the door, but Sax's bulk blocked the way. "Excuse me, Sax," she said.

He didn't move, nor did he take his eyes from her face.

Angie looked at him coldly. That he was a bully she already knew; now, belatedly, she realized that he was also dangerous.

"Get out of my way, Sax," she said evenly. "The skipper is waiting for me."

Sax's thick upper lip curled into a sneer. His dull eyes took on a cunning expression. "Huh," he jeered. "Now how come that don't s'prise me?"

He shifted imperceptibly aside. With a shudder of distaste, Angie held her breath and slid past him, trying not to let any part of her body touch his. Then putting him out of her mind, she ran down the deck, sprinted up the ladder to the speedboat deck and skidded to a halt at the door of the bridge. Through the wraparound windows she could see Joseph. He was standing in the wheelhouse, wearing earphones and speaking into a radio microphone.

He didn't hear her hesitant knock. When she pushed open the door and walked in, he barely took notice. He only looked up abstractedly and gestured at a chair, indicating that she should sit down, and so she did.

Minutes went by. Angie watched the flickering digital lights of the instrument panel, as well as the man whose attention was fixed on them with total concentration. At his fingertips was an abalone shell filled with cigarette butts and, as she watched, he reached over and stubbed out another one.

He paced back and forth between the tonnage gauge and the knobs that controlled the massive crane. He was still wearing his hard hat and his rubber seaboots, which slapped awkwardly against his legs as he moved. Angie wondered why he had them on at all. Then it dawned on her.

It could only mean he had been prepared to go into the net after her!

She groaned guiltily and slouched deeper into her chair. How many times had she heard Cappy, relaxed and mellow after a few glasses of Madeira, sermonize on the gospel of life on the high seas? A simple philosophy that hadn't changed significantly since Fletcher Christian and his mutineers seized *The Bounty* from Captain Bligh?

The skipper's word is law. He was responsible for everything that happened, both good and bad, aboard his vessel. If the catch was good, it was credited to him; if it was poor, it was his fault. He was responsible for the actions of his crew, and for any injuries or fatalities that occurred aboard his ship, even if he, himself, was not on board.

Angie groaned again. Joseph had no way of knowing that she was proficient at any shipboard tasks except cooking. He probably thought she was playing fast and loose with both her life and his reputation. It bothered her more than she would have thought possible that he might think her reckless, or worse yet, dumb.

She should have discussed the situation with him before she approached Dominic—Cappy had trained her better than that! She pushed herself upright in the chair and squared her shoulders, prepared to accept without complaint any disciplinary action he chose to impose. She deserved it.

For the first time, she felt a niggling doubt about her ability to run Reno Fisheries. There were a great many things about life in the fleet that she couldn't possibly know; now she wondered uneasily whether the business skills she had learned in college would truly compensate for that lack.

The radio had stopped its sporadic crackling. Angie became aware that the skipper's terse monologue had ended. She looked up to find him sitting at his desk, entering tonnage into the computer. When his computations were finished, he leaned back in his chair and clasped his hands behind his neck.

"We've got fifty thousand dollars of prime yellow-fin packed away in those wells," he announced cheerfully, regarding her with a satisfied smile. "Not bad for a morning's work, is it!"

Angie stood. "Skipper..." she began apprehensively.

He motioned her back down, then pivoted his chair toward her. He propped the ankle of one leg on the knee of the other and pulled off his seaboot, tossing it aside with a sigh of relief.

"Hot," he remarked.

Angie didn't know whether he meant the boots, or his foot or simply the weather. Her apprehension increased while he pulled off the other boot and tossed it on top of the first.

"Skipper..." she began again.

"Reno..." he said at the same time. When she stopped, flustered, he motioned to her to continue.

"Well, sir..." she said gingerly, uncertain how to proceed now that she had the floor.

"We can dispense with the *sir,* I think, Reno. I have the feeling we're long past that by now."

"Yes, sir," she said automatically. "I just wanted to say that I know I shouldn't have gone into the net without consulting you. I was wrong. And I'm sorry."

She recited the words quickly, like a memorized speech she was eager to get out of the way. Then she waited for his response. She knew that he had several options: he could confine her to quarters, he could dock her pay, he could even fire her and put her ashore at the first opportunity.

Instead he smiled. "You're not very good at apologies, are you, Reno?"

Angie looked at him blankly. "Pardon me?"

"Haven't you ever noticed that when most people apologize for something, they at least make an attempt to *sound* sorry? You don't. You sound as though you don't give a damn whether I accept your apology or not."

Angie's jaw tightened. "I don't understand what you mean."

"I mean that I don't think you could humble yourself if you tried. I mean that you're every bit as stubborn and every bit as proud as Long Jack was. In fact, you look a lot like him, sitting there with your jaw jutting out like that. That's what's called leading with your chin, Reno, and it's generally not considered the best way to defend yourself. In a barroom brawl you'd hit the floor before you could get your first punch off."

Angie made a conscious effort to relax her clenched teeth. "I wouldn't know," she said tartly. "I haven't had much experience with barroom brawls. Besides, most people tell me that I look just like my mother."

"Well, I wouldn't know about that." Joseph's voice was noncommittal. With the toe of one foot he swiveled his chair around to the front to look out over the foredeck. The sky was a sun-washed shade of blue, which the water reflected and deepened to the inky color of indigo. The *Sea Witch* swayed on its gentle swells like a cradle in the wind.

"Look, Reno," Joseph said, decisively swiveling back to look at Angie. "Let's make a deal, you and I. You stop trying to prove to me that you're an able-bodied seaman, and I'll stop trying to prove to you that you're not." He smiled. "What do you say?"

"I'm not trying to prove anything."

His eyebrows arched skeptically.

"Not to you." She lifted her chin, aware that her jaw was once again jutting forward argumentatively.

"Only to yourself?"

"Something like that."

"And maybe to your father?"

Angie eyed him indignantly. "Why on earth would I have anything to prove to Cappy?" she sputtered.

"I'm not sure. You tell me. Maybe that you're just as good as any son he might have had? Or maybe—that you can operate Reno Fisheries as well as any man?"

"I *am*," Angie replied to his first question, "and I *can*," to his second. "And I'll forego the two-bit psychoanalysis, if you don't mind."

"Of course," Joseph said gravely. "It's no concern of mine. But if it were..." He paused. "If it *were*, I'd tell you that you're one gutsy lady, and I'm glad to have you aboard."

Before Angie could register her astonishment, he swiveled his chair toward the foredeck once more, dismissing her.

"That'll be all, Reno," he said in a casual tone. "Oh, and one more thing. If I ever catch you pulling any more damn fool stunts like the one you pulled today, I'll bounce your fanny off my boat at the nearest port and let you find your own way back to San Diego!"

Chapter Nine

"Boat I was on once," said one of the fishermen, gulping a cup of coffee without even noticing that it was scalding, "—the *Calypso*, out of Dago, she was— we caught fifteen-hundred ton in one week. Only slept when we *fell* down. That was workin', let me tell you!"

"Boat I was on last year set six times in one day," said another. "Thirty hours straight! Now *that* was working!"

The men had labored sixteen hours without a break. Too keyed up to sleep, they gathered around the galley table, rehashing the events of the day, comparing them to other great sets they had known.

"Ye call yer'selves fishermen!" Dominic scoffed. "Back in the old line-and-pole days—back when fishin' was a *man's* job!—once I hooked into a three-pole bluefin, and I tell you, that tuna tailwalked just like a damned trout! Aint seen nothin' like it since! Thought he'd reel *me* in, 'stead o' the other way around! Landed 'im, finally. Threw 'im over my shoulder—"

"Old man's been reading again. Hemingway this time, sounds like to me!" Tennessee volunteered in his molasses-thick drawl.

"Old man," needled Show Biz. "The best day of your life, you never landed no three-poler!"

"It was with ol' Jack Reno!" Dominic appealed to Angie. "Tell 'em, girl! I know yer grandaddy must'a told ye about it—man dont fergit a thing like that!"

Angie grinned at him from her chair tipped back against the wall. "Sorry, Dominic! He never mentioned it to me."

One by one the men came down off their adrenaline high, stubbed out their cigarettes and headed for the fo'c'sle. Soon only Dominic and Sax remained—Dominic with his chin buried on his chest, snoring in deep exhaustion, and Sax staring moodily out the porthole across the room.

After a few minutes of silence, broken only by Dominic's explosive snores, Sax turned his pale eyes in Angie's direction. "Did'ja see me today?" he asked.

"You were good today, Sax. Everyone said so."

"Yeah, but did *you* see me?"

"Sure I did." What did he want her to say? "You were good," Angie repeated.

"I should'na said what I said to you the other day." His voice was as surly as ever. "Hell, I know you aint makin' it with the skipper."

"Thanks, Sax," she said. "I'm glad to hear that." If this was his idea of an apology, she thought with some amusement, it would have to do. It was certainly more than she'd expected. With a *thud,* she returned the front legs of her chair to the floor. "Is there something else you need, Sax?" she asked. "If not..." She yawned.

Sax rolled his pack of Marlboro cigarettes into the sleeve of his T-shirt. He picked up his lighter emblazoned with a nude woman outlined in rhinestones and shoved it into his back pocket. Then he prodded the dozing Dominic with a sharp elbow to the ribs.

"C'mon, old man," he growled, and lurched out the door.

Dominic struggled to his feet, his body obviously stiff and aching. "Gettin' too old for this kind'a thing," he mumbled as he followed Sax into the darkness.

IT WAS SOMETIME after midnight when Angie woke. For a moment she wasn't sure what had wakened her. It was the door, she thought sleepily; it was the rusty hinge that needed oil, squeaking like fingernails on a blackboard.

Angie rolled over and burrowed deeper into her pillow; then it occurred to her sleep-drugged mind that the door had never opened by itself before. She struggled toward consciousness. Instinctively pulling the thin sheet up to her chin as though for protection, she lay motionless and listening in the dark.

There was no light in the windowless little storeroom, only the blue streak of starlight that filtered in through the crack in the door, which slowly disappeared as the door creaked shut. The room was plunged into total darkness, but Angie sensed that it wasn't empty. She felt the icy chill of imminent danger.

Something damp and rough brushed her foot. She jerked the foot away, only to feel that same something fasten onto her ankle and begin to slide slowly, inexorably, up the calf of her leg. A shadow blacker than the other blackness in the cabin rose from the end of the bunk and loomed over her.

She froze. A scream lodged in her throat, shriveling into nothing more than a tiny, terrified whimper by the time it broke through. She began to scramble backward on the bed, step by panic-stricken step. Her breath came in short, sharp pants.

"Who's there?" she demanded in a cracked whisper. The black shadow came closer. *"Who's there?"*

"It's me. It's Sax. Don't make any noise."

Sax! Angie shoved him aside, leapt from the bunk and flung open the door. She made a wild dash for the galley hatch, only to find that Sax had thrown the dead bolt. She clawed desperately at it, panic making her hands clumsy.

Glancing feverishly over her shoulder, she saw that Sax was nearly on top of her. Even in the dim blue starlight streaming in through the galley's two portholes, she could make out his eyes. They were staring, not at her face but at the neckline of her nightshirt, where the parting of her breasts began.

Not shifting his gaze, Sax grabbed at the collar, ripping the nightshirt down the front. Buttons flew in all directions. One huge ham hand grabbed greedily at her. Angie ducked under his upraised arm and fled across the room.

"I'll scream," she warned, even though the terror rising in her throat wouldn't permit her anything more than a hoarse whisper.

"Go 'head," Sax growled with a menacing sneer. "For all the good it'll do ye. Everyone's out cold, dead to the world after the fishin'. No one's gonna hear ye."

"The skipper. His cabin's right above—he'll hear."

"I dont think so. But what if he does? He aint gonna stop me, not even if he could. Hell, he'll prob'ly get in line right behind me!"

With her eyes fixed on his like a deer caught in the headlights of an oncoming truck, Angie backed slowly around the long table. Too late she felt the corner at her back, and realized that she had nowhere else to go.

Talk, she told herself. *Reason with him!* "You'll never get away with this, Saxby. Think! Where will you go? There's no place on this boat you'll be able to hide—!"

"Who's gonna believe ye? Prancin' around a bunch of sex-starved bastids like you was the Queen of Sheba—?" He licked his lips like a predator closing in on its prey. "Besides, ye want it. I know ye do. Ye watched me today." His voice was low and brutal. "Ye need a man. And it aint that pretty-boy skipper ye need, neither!"

Inch by imperceptible inch, Angie had been creeping along the bulkhead. Before Sax realized what she was doing, she reached for the liquor locker and threw it open, fitting her shaking fingers around the neck of a whiskey bottle. One frantic motion and she had pulled it out and smashed it against the edge of the Formica. The stench of spilled whiskey was nauseating.

"Don't, Sax!" she warned, brandishing the jagged neck of the broken bottle in front of her face. "I mean it."

Angie didn't have time to slash at him with the razor-sharp glass; she didn't even have time to consider it. Sax vaulted over the table. He seized her wrist and slammed it high against a cupboard door. Pinning her against the counter with his full weight, he pulled her head back by a hank of hair and forced her mouth open against his. It was impossible to breathe without taking in the staleness he exhaled, and Angie's breath came in gasps as she struggled desperately for oxygen.

This can't be happening! she shrieked in her mind, choking as his thick tongue rammed itself down her throat. *Not this! Not me!* She thought for a despairing instant of Joseph, just a few feet above them. Then her body went rigid with helpless terror as she felt the hard bulge of his crotch against her stomach.

Suddenly there was the crash of breaking glass. Sax whirled his head to look over his shoulder. Angie, her mouth freed, fell against the counter, drinking in huge, choking gulps of air.

The hatch porthole lay in shattered pieces on the floor, and an arm was reaching through the jagged hole to unlock the dead bolt. Then, with a violent kick, the door burst open. In the blue starlight stood Joseph. There was a fire ax in his hand and the wrath of God on his face. He switched on the light.

Sax began to edge away. He slunk fearfully along the bulkheads, his unblinking eyes glued to Joseph's face. His own face had turned a sickly shade of gray, and his labored breathing was fast and shallow. No longer predator, now he was prey, desperately seeking an escape from a situation his instincts had already recognized as hopeless.

A few feet from Joseph he stopped, uncertain which way he should try to bolt. His eyes darted to one side— not even a movement, just the thought of movement; Joseph lifted his arm and Sax fell back, cowering. He licked his dry lips.

"Skipper," he whined placatingly. "It aint what ye think. She wanted me to come. She *asked* me to!"

"Enough!" Joseph roared. "Enough," he repeated after a malevolent pause, and his voice was dangerously calm. It sounded more threatening than the roar. "Get back to the fo'c'sle. Stay there. We'll be in Puntarenas in three days—I'll put you ashore there. If you come anywhere near her again, I'll kill you."

There was no rage in his voice. It was just a bald, unemotional statement of fact.

"But—what about my share, Skipper?" Sax whined. "I gotta get my share...."

"Talk to your union when you get back to Dago—*if* you get back to Dago. I hear any more about your share, I'll have you up on charges so fast, you won't know what hit you." Contemptuously he stepped aside just far enough to allow the man to squeeze out the door.

Like a crab, Sax crouched and scurried. When he reached the place where Joseph stood, he put on a burst of speed that caused him to stumble and fall on all fours in the broken glass from the porthole. He didn't even slow down. His eyes remained fixed on Joseph's until he was safely out of the door; then his footsteps pounded on the deck as he turned tail and ran.

Joseph turned to Angie. "You all right?" he asked gravely.

She nodded.

He jutted his chin toward the jagged neck of the whiskey bottle she still clutched in her hand. "Where did a Portuguese princess learn a trick like that?"

Angie looked at the glass as though she'd never seen it before; then she opened her fingers as if it had burned her and let it fall to the floor. "Cappy," she said. "He could never decide whether he wanted me to be a son or a daughter, so he made me a little bit of both."

"Would you really have cut him?"

"Yes."

"Good!"

Angie began to tremble uncontrollably. Suddenly she was nauseated, and she doubled over from sharp cramps in her stomach. Swiftly Joseph moved to her side. He held her shoulders as she retched violently.

"It's all over now," he crooned, hugging her loosely as she clung to him, sobbing—harsh, dry, ugly sobs that wracked her body.

When the sobs finally subsided, he held her shoulders and scanned her quickly from head to foot, reassuring himself that she was unhurt. When he looked down, he was appalled to see that she was standing amidst shards of broken glass that floated in a pool of whiskey on the floor.

"Your feet!" he exclaimed. With his hands around her waist, he lifted her as easily as though she were no heavier than a small child and sat her down on top of the counter. He pulled his T-shirt over his head with a single, lithe twist of his torso, then hunkered down on his heels and used it to brush the slivers of glass from the bottoms of her feet.

"Your poor feet," he chided again very softly, speaking as much to himself as to Angie.

Watching from her perch on the countertop, Angie was amazed to see streaks of blood on the cloth. "I didn't even feel it," she said wonderingly.

When Joseph thought that all the glass had been brushed away, he stood and dropped the T-shirt onto the floor. He wrapped the tails of the torn nightshirt tightly around Angie and hefted her into his arms with no more effort than if she truly *had* been a child.

She clung to his neck as he turned and headed for the door. She didn't know where he was taking her, but instinctively she knew that wherever it was, she would be safe.

A SINGLE LAMP BURNED in Joseph's quarters. A leather couch extended the full length of the bulkhead at one end of the cabin, and it was to the couch that Joseph carried Angie and gently deposited her. He tucked the tails of her nightshirt under her knees, then sat down beside her and took her once more into his arms.

With infinite tenderness, he softly smoothed the disheveled hair back from her face. "You're all right now," he repeated over and over again like a soothing mantra. "Everything's going to be all right."

Angie was stiff in his arms. She could still feel the ugliness of Sax's coarse eyes scraping her body, and his mouth at her throat. She could still feel the helpless, hopeless vulnerability. Abruptly, her thin veneer of composure crumbled and with a long, shuddering moan she slumped heavily against Joseph, weak with relief and gratitude.

"There, there," he continued in the same quiet, nonthreatening tone. He leaned back into the leather cushions and drew Angie back with him, so that she lay almost in his lap. "Everything's going to be all right," he murmured. "I'll never let anything hurt you."

His breath, so close to her ear, tickled the curls that floated in wispy tendrils around her face, and the thick mat of dark hair on his chest made a soft pillow for her head. Lying still in his arms, Angie could hear the steady beating of his heart, and somehow it calmed her.

"I don't know what to say," she began tentatively after a while, her words muffled by the pillow of his hair. "I don't know how to thank you...."

"No need. Just doing my job." She felt as well as heard his voice rumble from deep in his chest. His hands stopped smoothing her hair back from her forehead and reached down to tilt her face upward. "Are you all right now?"

Reluctantly Angie sat up. She smiled tremulously, then self-consciously wrapped her torn nightshirt more tightly around herself.

Joseph understood. He rose and left the room, returning a moment later with a blue terry-cloth robe, which he held out to her. He kept his back turned as he walked to his tiny kitchenette at the other end of the cabin, where he began rummaging through the lockers.

Angie climbed into the commodious robe, grateful for both Joseph's sensitivity and his discretion. She curled into a corner of the couch, drawing up her legs with the robe secured modestly around them.

For the first time since she had come into it, Angie took notice of the cabin. These company boats had luxuries unheard of in Cappy's day, she thought. The walls were paneled in rich walnut, and thick blue carpet covered the floor.

There were few personal touches: a stack of books on the floor, two photographs taped to the mirror above the couch. One was a black-and-white snapshot of a middle-aged couple—his parents?—smiling into the sun; the other, a faded color photograph of two young boys—himself? and a brother, maybe?—sitting in the crook of a tree, each holding a fishing pole with its line dangling somewhere beneath the camera's lens.

Joseph came back into the room, carrying a bottle and two brandy snifters. Angie took the goblet he offered her. He half filled hers and then his own with brandy from the bottle, then folded his long body onto the opposite end of the couch.

Angie held the bowl of the snifter between her cupped hands. She swirled the golden liquid around while her downcast eyes studied the ripples in the bottom of the glass. Would she ever be able to look Joseph in the eye again, she wondered? Her glance flickered up to meet his, shyly looked away, then irresistibly flickered back.

"Drink up," he said, and smiled at her over the rim of his glass. "It's good medicine."

The brandy was very potent. It burned Angie's throat all the way down, and hit her stomach like liquid fire. "Strong," she ventured.

"It's from my own vineyard," Joseph said, a note of pride in his voice.

Angie glanced at the imprinted label on the bottle. "Montero?"

"Well, not mine *literally*. It comes with the territory, I guess you could say."

"Montero's takes very good care of its skippers," she observed.

That was the last thing she observed that night.

The brandy worked its magic. Despite the violent emotions of the last hour, or perhaps because of them, Angie felt its heady effect almost immediately. Joseph's face, with its angles and planes and the cleft in the chin that was almost a scar, kept going in and out of focus, drifting closer and then floating away.

Angie blinked rapidly a few times, struggling to remember who he was and who she was, and why she was here. Joseph held out his arms and sleepily, as trustingly as a child, she crept into them.

With a hatred that was irrational but all-consuming, he thought about the man who had put her there, the man who thought he could take by force what Joseph himself had hardly dared dream of. Something atavistic in him hoped that Sax would defy Joseph's edict so that Joseph could carry out the threat he had made.

Angie stirred briefly, unconsciously nestling closer. "Joseph," she murmured sleepily. "It means...good caretaker... But I knew that...I knew it all along." Then her eyelids fluttered closed again, the lashes sweeping thick and dark above her flushed cheeks, and gave every indication of staying that way.

"Not so good," Joseph said almost to himself, as he softly stroked her hair. His voice was bleak. "We're not so different, Saxby and I. And may God damn me for it."

He looked down at her, tear tracks still evident on her sleeping face. Reluctantly his eyes flickered lower, to the gap between the lapels of the blue robe. He saw the shadowed valley between her breasts, and the fullness of one as it rose to a breathtaking point. He stared hungrily, unable to make himself look away.

The ivory curves, pale in contrast to the tanned flesh that surrounded them, rose and fell with Angie's measured breathing. Their heaviness rested on Joseph's arm as he held her sleeping form. His fingers ached to explore the swelling roundness; he kept them where they were. His lips ached to fit themselves over the delicate brown tip; he kissed her temple where it rested against his jaw.

He thought again of Sax, and he was ashamed. Deliberately he tucked the terry-cloth robe up to Angie's chin. Gazing downward avidly but shamefacedly, he watched the tantalizing curve of her breast disappear as his reluctant fingers folded the wide blue lapels over it.

He held her cautiously, gingerly, as if she would break if he held her too tightly. Or as if he would.

Chapter Ten

Sunlight filtered through the salt-encrusted glass of the porthole. Angie stretched luxuriously, until she remembered that there was no sunlight in her cabin, nor room in her bunk to stretch.

Her eyes snapped open, wide and for a moment confused. Then memories of the night before came flooding back, beginning with the door creaking open in her cabin, and ending with the glass of brandy she had drunk much too quickly.

She fought the almost irresistible urge to crawl back beneath the blanket and hide. Instead she sat up in the unfamiliar bed, and discovered that she was alone in a bedroom she had never seen before. She also discovered that she was still wearing Joseph's terry-cloth robe, which had bunched uncomfortably beneath her while she slept. She swung her legs over the side of the bed and stood, straightening the robe and tightening the sash at her waist.

The lush blue carpet beneath her feet told her that this bedroom had to be part of Joseph's quarters; and indeed, it was every bit as spartan as the blue-carpeted main cabin she remembered from last night. A rough brown blanket was all that covered the bed, and there was only one skinny pillow.

Across the room she saw a set of silver-backed brushes lined up on a bureau. They were ornately carved, and their soft sheen told Angie that they could only be sterling.

She walked to the bureau and picked up the brushes one at a time, turning them over in her hand and examining them thoughtfully. They said something about the man who owned them, she concluded. One, that he had a taste for the luxury of fine, rich things, and two, that he didn't indulge that taste often, for the silver brushes were the only luxurious touches in the otherwise ascetic room.

Next to the brushes on the bureau was a small stack of clothing, which proved upon closer inspection to be jeans and a work shirt from her own cabin. Looking down, she saw her sneakers placed neatly side by side on the floor.

A miniscule bathroom was adjacent to the bedroom, and suddenly Angie was overcome by an urgent need to shower. She twisted on the faucet in the shower stall full blast. The water was hot, almost hotter than she could bear; but it felt good, too, and as she scrubbed with the bar of soap she found hanging from the shower head, she felt that she was washing away the feel of Sax's eyes on her body, and the touch of his grasping, sausagelike fingers.

When the water turned cold, she dried herself with the coarse white towel hanging behind the door, then she slipped into the clothes Joseph had provided and walked out into the main cabin.

Eat, instructed a note on the breakfast bar. *"I'll be back as soon as I can.*

Angie examined the contents of the refrigerator and decided that she wasn't the least bit hungry. But following instructions, she popped a slice of bread into the toaster, spread it with butter and jam, and poured a glassful of orange juice. She had just finished the last bite of toast when the door opened and Joseph walked in.

"How are you feeling this morning, Reno?" he asked casually, as if it were the most natural thing in the world to find a woman seated at his breakfast bar.

"I'm fine, Skipper," she replied. Suddenly she was overcome with the same shyness that had affected her the night before. She glanced at him quickly and then focused her attention on organizing the crumbs on her plate into neat little piles with her finger. "About last night..." Her tongue didn't seem to be cooperating this morning, so she took a deep breath and began again. "Last night...I mean, I have to thank you...."

He made a dismissive gesture with one hand. "That's not necessary. I'm just glad that nothing more serious happened."

His voice was pleasant and impersonal. Angie saw that he was maintaining the proper working relationship between them, not reminding her by words or attitude of the forced intimacies of last night. An honorable man, she told herself gratefully. A *conquistador.*

"We'll make Costa Rica in a week," Joseph continued. "If you want to press charges, I'll radio ahead and have the local police meet us at the dock."

"No!" Angie shuddered. "No," she said again more quietly. "I just want to forget it. As you said, nothing serious happened...."

"That's not what I said. I said, 'nothing *more* serious happened.' What happened was bad enough—but you and I both know that it certainly could have been worse." He looked at her thoughtfully. "Of course it's up to you. But this probably isn't the first time he's done something like this. If someone had brought him up on charges before, he might not have been around to—"

"All right! I'll do it. But, please, I just don't want to talk about it anymore!"

"What are you ashamed of, Angeli?" he demanded, using her given name for the first time since she'd come aboard his boat.

He propped one foot on the rung of the stool where she sat and caught her chin between thumb and forefinger, tilting her face upward so that she had no choice but to look directly into his eyes. "Listen up! You have nothing to be ashamed of. Do you hear me? Nothing!"

Angie found unexpected comfort in his words and his touch. "I know. I just feel so...*stupid,* that's all! I never thought..."

"The only problem you have is in thinking that all fishermen are like your father. They're not. *We're* not. Take precautions from now on." He fixed her with a stern gaze. "I've nailed some boards across the broken window—now *you* make sure you lock the door every night. *With* the dead bolt. Do you understand?"

Angie nodded. She seemed to be having some trouble speaking this morning, but maybe that was just as well, because she wasn't sure she could express in words the things she was feeling.

Gratitude, of course, but it was more than that. She remembered the arm reaching through the shattered porthole to unlock the dead bolt. Even before she had seen his face, she had known who it was. She had sensed it somehow. And the unquestioning trust she had felt when he scooped her up in his arms and carried her to the safe cocoon of his cabin had remained with her all night.

It was with her now, as she smiled up at him and realized that every trace of embarrassment had vanished. "I can't believe I slept right through breakfast," she said.

"You needed it," Joseph replied.

"The men must be starving...."

"Dominic did the honors this morning. And I have a feeling everyone's going to be real glad to see you back."

"Well, then, I guess I'd better get started on lunch," Angie said, turning to go. But at the door she stopped and looked around. "And, thanks. For everything."

Joseph flashed his professional "skipper" smile. "Just doing my job," he said.

JOSEPH KNEW the superstitious fishermen believed that *mav sorte*—bad luck—came in threes. First there was the matter of losing one of the diesels at the beginning of the season. Then there was the matter of sailing with a woman on board and subsequently losing their number-one speedboat driver. And now there was the matter of the fish. They seemed to have played out.

Joseph spent long hours on the glasses, and when he came down from the crow's nest, even the whites of his eyes were sunburned. But there was no sign of fish.

Near the end of the fifth fishless day, Joseph spotted a few porpoises due east. It looked insignificant but, falling farther and farther behind, he decided to go for it. He ordered the speedboats launched.

That they were in trouble was apparent almost immediately.

Pinheiro, promoted to Number One, was overly cautious. He operated his boat tentatively, and it wasn't possible to drive a speedboat with anything less than brash confidence. The novice assigned to Number Five kept getting ahead of the others, zigging when he should have zagged, and zagging when he should have zigged.

The wind suddenly shifted, keeping the skiff starboard when it tried to circle to port. The crew had to set the net blind, and the whole thing ended up a lot of work for a very small return. The men, when they gathered in the galley for supper, were surly and unsociable.

The next day was more promising. The weather was calm, and Joseph sighted a number of porpoises just after first light. Tense and edgy, the crew was eager to prove that the previous day's failure had been a fluke. However, as soon as the speedboats took off, it was evident that they were in trouble again.

Pinheiro had lost whatever measure of confidence he'd had, and he held back so hard on his throttle that he swamped his boat. Number Three developed engine trouble and had to return to the *Sea Witch*, leaving only four boats to work the school. It wasn't enough. By the time the skiff hit the water, the school had gone deep. In disgust, Joseph radioed the speedboats and aborted the set.

If the men had been surly before, they were spoiling for a fight now. In an ugly mood they gathered in the fo'c'sle, and not even Dominic's wry humor could distract them.

After a few hours of escalating tension, a group broke off and went topside to the bridge.

"Cap'n," said their appointed spokesman, after he had requested and been granted permission to enter. "We dont want any more trouble—"

"Neither do I," Joseph returned shortly.

"Cap'n, there aint no point to Sax just sittin' there in his bunk. We need him, Cap'n. With Pinheiro ridin' Number One, we aint never gonna get nothin' done out here."

"Give Pinheiro a chance. He hasn't been at it long enough. With a little more experience, he'll be fine."

"Sure he will, Skipper," broke in another man. "But it wont be in time to do us any good. We came out here to fish. If we aint gonna fish, what're we doing out here? Beggin' your pardon, sir."

The leader, a brailer with almost as much time in the fleet as Dominic, spoke again. "Now, we all know what Sax is," he said reasonably. "But whatever else he is, he's one hell of a speedboat driver. Without him, we're like to go home with empty wells."

Tennessee, standing beside the leader, interrupted. "We want you to give him his old job back." His slow drawl was a boyish wheedle. "Just for now. Just 'til we get to Puntarenas."

"I call this mutiny, mister," Joseph said dangerously.

"No sir!" the leader assured him. "Just tellin' you how we feel. We're fishermen—we gotta fish to take care of our people, that's all."

"Montero's will make good on your shares, no matter what the boat does," Joseph countered.

"It ain't that, Cap'n," the man said stubbornly. "It's just—it's our job. It's what we are."

Joseph faced the nervous group with icy authority. Behind him stood only Madruga, and Otis, the navigator. They both looked as jittery as the rest of the crew.

"You've made your opinions known, and they're duly noted. Now get out. And any man jack who wants to challenge me aboard my own boat had better have the guts to back it up!"

"College man," growled one deckhand disdainfully, as the group about-faced and shuffled off the bridge. "Learned how to fish from a friggin' book!"

"Company man," another groused. "Never got his hands dirty in his life!"

Impassively, Joseph watched them go; then he turned to Madruga. "You've got the bridge," he ordered curtly. "I'll be on the glasses."

After he'd left, Madruga looked at Otis, his long, gaunt face even more cadaverous than usual.

"They got a point," he ventured.

Otis just shrugged.

Chapter Eleven

The brawl took Angie by surprise.

Only when she saw deckhands racing excitedly past the galley and heard the sound of footsteps pounding topside did she realize something was very wrong. She looked at Luis, whose blank black eyes mirrored her own. Then she ran out of the galley, the sullen cookboy hot on her heels.

Arriving on the speedboat deck, what she saw hit her like a fist to the stomach.

The crew had cleared the deck around Joseph, who was striding purposefully toward the Number One speedboat. Angie elbowed her way to the front of the crowd, and in a few terse words, one of the men filled her in.

Joseph had been up the mast, from which he had radioed the dolphin sighting. But instead of orchestrating the fishing from the crow's nest, as he normally would have done, he had ordered Madruga to the glasses while he himself went to the speedboat deck.

By the time Angie arrived, the speedboats were ready to be launched and the men were tense, for Pinheiro was back in the second boat and Sax was strapping on the radio headset in Number One.

As Joseph approached, Sax eyed him with an expression of sly, animal cunning. "Looks like I got my old job back, Skipper," he said with a smirk.

Looking at Joseph, Angie shivered involuntarily. His face wore a glacial calmness, and his narrow eyes slitted dangerously—telltale bits of body language that only Angie recognized as outrage, and only because she had seen it before, then as now directed at Sax.

Incredibly, Sax himself didn't seem to recognize the fury in Joseph's face, either. His smirk widened triumphantly as he raised his arm to give the "lower away" signal to the crane operator. Unprepared for Joseph's move, a murmur of admiration rippled over the assembled men when he hauled Sax out of Number One and threw him flat on the deck.

Sax grunted when he hit, then rolled fast and got his feet back under him. He hunkered down in a crouch, brandishing his fists in front of his face, jabbing the air like a shadow boxer. He circled Joseph, looking for an opening.

Sax was big but he was slow, and before he could throw a punch, Joseph was on him. He jerked Sax upright, then caught him with a hard left to the stomach, followed by the sickening crunch of a right to the jaw.

Sax went down with a sound like air *swooshing* out of a balloon, and this time he stayed down.

"Confine him to quarters," Joseph ordered no one in particular. Two astonished deckhands came forward, seized Sax under his arms and dragged him away.

Joseph climbed into Number One. He fastened the life jacket and kidney belt around his midsection, then retrieved the headset he had snatched from Sax and strapped it over his head. With an incisive downward thrust of his thumb, he signaled the crane operator to lower away.

Stunned, Angie joined Dominic at the rail. "What brought that on?" she demanded.

Briefly Dominic described the confrontation that had taken place on the bridge that morning. "'Course I wasn't there," he concluded. "But I hear tell the skipper leaned on 'em pretty hard. Hope he aint gonna regret it."

"But he couldn't go back on his word. Don't the men understand that?"

"It aint just a matter of confinin' Sax to quarters, not anymore. He shamed Sax in front of his *compadres*—Sax aint never gonna fergit that. And now the skipper's gonna ride Number One hisself. I don't mind tellin' ye, Angie girl—I don't like it. I don't like it one bit."

"Maybe he should have let Pinheiro have another chance at it," Angie theorized uneasily. "Pinheiro's been driving speedboats almost as long as Saxby—"

"Pinheiro's got eyes for Number One, all right, but he aint got the guts for it. Look for yerself, Angie girl!"

Angie's uneasy eyes followed the sweep of Dominic's arm as he gestured at the whitecaps all around them. A hot, gusty wind from a tropical depression to the east was keeping the surface roiling, even though the sky was clear.

"See what I mean?" he continued. "Anything more than three, four foot, it's rough goin' for the speedboats. Those swells, they're ten foot, easy. And the wind's thirty knots. If the skipper wasn't gonna let Sax work, he should'n'a called a set in this weather. Aint but a half-dozen men could lead the boats in seas like this. Saxby's one. . . ."

Apprehensively, Angie focused her attention on the tiny flotilla of aluminum boats. "The skipper... *isn't?*"

"Not so's I ever heard. Well, hell, he's still wet behind the *ears!* He aint had the *time*—"

Suddenly his words were drowned out by shouts from the other crewmen lined up at the rail. Dominic cursed, and crossed himself.

Number One was airborne. It seemed to pause for a breathtaking moment between the pale sky and the darker sea; then it cleared the churning wake and began zigzagging toward the horizon. One by one, the other boats followed Joseph as he searched for the safest routes of passage. They looked like toys, rising on the crest of a wave and then disappearing into the ten-foot troughs of another.

Along with everyone else, Angie was glued to the rail, as astounded as they by what was simply the most daring display of speedboat driving any of them had ever witnessed.

Joseph never made a false move, nor an unnecessary one. Serpentining, he led the boats out beyond the school of yellowfin, where the five positioned themselves in an enormous semicircle and began herding the fish closer and closer to the *Sea Witch.*

A swell advanced on him, and then another; rolling hills of gray-blue marble laced with white veins—ponderous, ominous, alive with some primal purpose of their own. The wind caught the underside of his tiny boat and lifted its bow so high that it was vertical to the water, then bounced it back down with a bone-jarring slam.

Joseph looked like some kind of ancient sea god, Angie thought in awe—like Neptune, maybe, or Poseidon or even Davy Jones himself. One arm reached backward to angle the outboard, and the other stretched forward to the steering wheel. He was one with his boat, its power seeming to run through his body like an electric current.

Angie felt what she knew he must be feeling—the excitement, the exhilaration, the wild, sweet thrill of conquest as he rode with imperious arrogance on the unwilling shoulders of the sea.

And she knew how he must look—the air whistling past his headphone so loud, he could barely hear the radio, hair blowing straight back, eyes narrowed to slits from the sheer force of the wind. His lips would be drawn into a thin, hard line, and every muscle in his body straining with the effort of keeping the tiny boat on course.

He would be one with the elements. He would be home.

For as long as the speedboats bobbed like corks on the surface of the water, Angie watched them. The orange life jackets the men wore were visible long after the silver-gray of their boats had fused with the grayness of the sea.

The noise of a successful set raged on around her. She heard the rattling of the cables when Madruga ordered the skiff launched. After a time she heard the brailer kick into action, and the rude, exuberant voices of the men shouting obscenities at each other in their private pidgin.

The speedboats had done their job well. Angie could tell that the long run of *mav sorte* was over.

WHEN THE SPEEDBOATS had returned to the *Sea Witch* and been lifted aboard, Joseph pulled the radio headset from his head and tossed it to Pinheiro, who still sat in Number Two.

"*That's* the way you drive a speedboat," he said contemptuously.

He shrugged out of his life jacket and unfastened the waterlogged kidney belt. Then, just as though he were any other driver and not the skipper, he finished the job.

He passed cables over the bow and stern of Number One and secured them around giant cleats on either side of the deck. Then he hosed down the speedboat inside and out, and rinsed down the deck around it. He worked quickly, efficiently, balancing on the rolling deck with the easy, slightly bowlegged gait called "sea legs."

The tropical wind was hot. Joseph stripped to the waist for his task, and sweat mixed with seawater glistened on his skin. His biceps bulged as he tightened the speedboat into its mooring. The long muscles of his back rippled as he bent to attach the cables to the cleats, and the sun slid sinuously down his perspiring back, one vertebrae at a time.

From where she stood against the rail, Angie watched him, half-mesmerized. She found that she couldn't look away. Even if he had looked up and caught her gaze, and read in her eyes the unexpected stab of desire that was hotter than the hot afternoon sun beating down on them both, she would have been helpless to drag her eyes away.

His clumsy rubber seaboots were folded loosely below his knees and damp denim clung to his legs, outlining and defining them for her avid inspection. Soft black hair whorled wetly on his chest, and a smaller patch of the same dark hair curled on his flat stomach

and then disappeared into the waistband of his clinging jeans.

For as long as he worked, Angie was immobilized.
She had no choice but to remain where she was, studying him with hot, desirous eyes. Her hand gripped the
rail, tighter and tighter, until her knuckles turned
white. When he finished, she expelled a ragged breath
and drooped against the rail, as if his strong hands were
no longer holding her up.

Joseph reached for his shirt and put it on, rolling the
sleeves up past his elbows and leaving the front unbut-
toned. As he turned to go below, the sun glinted off
something hard and metallic around his neck.

Curious, Angie looked closer. She saw a narrow gold
chain, and suspended from it a small gold crucifix. His
price of admission, she thought with a sudden chill, to
Davy Jones's locker.

"I COULD FEED YOU GUYS bread and water tonight,"
Angie teased the men sitting around the table, "and
you probably wouldn't even notice!"

"That's so, Reno," returned Show Biz, without losing the rhythm of his chewing.

"—just as long as there's plenty of it," interrupted
Tennessee. Even his molasses-slow drawl sounded
boisterous.

But when Joseph came in from the bridge, an uneasy silence fell. Tennessee, who had been occupying
Joseph's chair at the head of the table, quickly vacated it. Every man's eyes fell to his plate, as if he
couldn't transfer food from there to his mouth without giving the procedure his undivided attention.

Furtively, though, everyone watched Joseph. They
had all heard how his authority had been challenged on

the bridge that morning, and no man knew him well enough to predict how he would handle it.

Joseph filled his plate from the enormous serving bowls in front of him and ate a few bites in silence. The tension in the room was almost palpable. Then he turned to the brailer who had been the one to issue the challenge.

"Nice piece of work out there today," he said gruffly.

A collective sigh of relief circled the table. The bull session picked up again. Joseph stuck an unlighted cigarette in the corner of his mouth; another crew member quickly offered a light. It was the signal for the poker game to begin.

"How about a refill, Reno?" Joseph said, holding his empty mug out to Angie without looking up.

Things were back to normal.

Chapter Twelve

The *Sea Witch* docked in the Costa Rican deep-water harbor of Thieves Bay, once a hideout for pirates, now a major port of call for the tuna fleet. Canneries lined the water's edge. Pungent fumes belched from the smokestacks on the roofs and drifted in charcoal billows out to sea.

The first thing the crew discovered upon docking was that Sax was gone. To avoid the *policia* he knew would be waiting for him, he had apparently gone over the side as soon as the diesels were shut down.

The rest of the crew left by more conventional means. Angie watched them as they crossed the gangplank in groups of two's and three's. Hair slicked back, showered and shaved, there was a spring in their steps and a gleam in their eyes. Twelve hours ashore—to men who spent most of their lives planning for their short sojourns ashore, it was almost an eternity.

Gypsies of the sea, Cappy used to call them. Sampling the feast of life at tables never even dreamed of by most men. Angie envied them. How wonderful, she thought, to walk into a café in Panama, a bar on the Gold Coast, a cantina in Costa Rica, and be welcomed like an old friend.

"Going ashore?"

It was Joseph. He wore white trousers, topped by a white crewneck sweater with the sleeves pushed up. Slung over one shoulder was a rumpled linen jacket, looking somewhat the worse for having traveled so far in a sea trunk. A yachtsman's cap was tilted rakishly over one eye.

Definitely one of the gypsies, Angie said to herself, smiling. "What does a *woman* do ashore?" she asked mischievously.

"Well-l-l . . . let's see." He appeared to consider the matter carefully. "I don't know," he said finally, puzzled. "The same things a man does, I guess."

Angie eyed him skeptically. "In a pig's eye!"

Joseph's eyes widened with feigned innocence. "What?" he protested.

"Oh, don't give me that innocent look, Captain Callais! I was born and *raised* in the fleet, remember?"

He grinned then, looking just the slightest bit sheepish. "Okay, we'll do whatever *women* like to do— this time. Shop. Visit the museums and art galleries— that sort of thing. What do you say?"

"Well . . ." She hesitated for a moment, remembering yesterday on the speedboat deck, when the sight of his nearly naked body shining like copper in the hot sun had nearly made her cry out with a pleasure that was almost as sharp as pain.

She had no doubts about him—he was the skipper, and it was obvious that he took the responsibility seriously. But she wasn't so sure about herself. She had been a very long time without . . . affection. *Affection* was the word she forced herself to use, but her fertile imagination painted a much more graphic picture; and into that picture it painted, not Mano, but Joseph.

"Yes, I'd like very much to go ashore with you," she finally decided, as if there had really been any doubt. "On one condition."

"And that is . . . ?"

"That we see something more . . . *exciting* than museums and art galleries. Actually, I saw those years ago, when I came here with my father. I don't think places like museums and art galleries change that much."

"Exciting it will be," he promised solemnly. "You have my word on it."

Draping one arm casually around Angie's shoulder, he escorted her across the gangplank, and into the heart of the brawling, bustling metropolis of Puntarenas.

Puntarenas was an old city, Angie remembered, as she and Joseph walked through the littered, fetid-smelling streets. And a dirty one. It had been old and dirty when Cappy first brought her here, and the intervening years hadn't improved it any.

Behind the dingy waterfront, the downtown area consisted of dismal, ramshackle structures and cheap flophouses. Bar after bar oozed drunks into the streets. This was the Puntarenas that greeted the gypsies of the world—the fishermen, the merchant mariners, the coffee brokers, the drifters. And they liked it because it was familiar, because it made no demands on them and because, no matter how long they'd been away, it never changed.

But there was another Puntarenas, which Angie discovered when Joseph hailed a taxi and instructed the driver to take them up into the hills.

This other Puntarenas had immaculate cobblestone streets, and picturesque alleys lined with shops offering everything from local batiks to elegant French perfume. This Puntarenas had intimate little restaurants built around courtyards where peacocks strutted and exotic tropical birds screamed in the gleaming, dark green banana trees.

The taxi let them out on a cobblestone street flanked by stone fences and white-washed houses with red tile roofs. It was *siesta,* and the street was empty except for a solitary vendor who hawked *cabrito,* iced coconuts and mangoes-on-a-stick from a brightly painted donkey cart.

When they reached the cart Joseph bought two iced coconuts, which the vendor sliced open with one sure stroke of a machete, then decorated with straws and skewers of fruit and, with a toothless smile, handed to them. Sipping the coconut milk, they explored the picturesque, old-fashioned village, strolling down steep, winding cobblestone streets that had once been goat paths.

"Hungry?" Joseph asked after a while.

By way of an iron gate half-hidden by woody bougainvillea vines, they stepped through a stone wall and emerged into another, fairy-tale world.

On the other side of the wall was an old café, all crumbling stucco and peeling paint, built around a tiny patio. It was shadowed from the hot afternoon sun by a thicket of glossy, dark green banana trees. The roots of enormous, ancient oaks broke through the clay tiles of the patio floor, and soft green moss grew between the cracks. Beneath the trees, a somnolent musician plucked desultorily at a mandolin.

An elderly maître d' with an ingratiating smile and a towel folded over his arm met them at the gate. He wore a tuxedo shirt, the top three studs left undone, and a black, none-too-clean waistcoat.

Obviously rattled by the extraordinary appearance of *norteamericanos* in his establishment, he smiled and bowed nervously, then smiled and bowed a few more times as he preceded Angie and Joseph to a wrought-iron table in the middle of the tiny patio.

Still smiling nervously, the maître d' cleared his throat politely. "*Y*…and…*para tomar*…to drink you would like…which?"

"Uh, *dos cafés, por favor,*" Joseph replied.

The maître d' raised his eyebrows heavenward, askance. "*El día*…the day *hace mucho calor*…it's very warm. *Ustedes están ciertos*…you are certain you want coffee?"

"*Perdóname,*" Joseph amended. "*Dos cafés fríos, por favor.*"

"Ah, *sí,* coffee *con* ice! *Sí!*" The maître d' looked relieved. He clapped his hands at someone out of sight on the patio. "*Dos cafés fríos!*" he ordered importantly.

Immediately a young waiter hustled across the courtyard. Struggling into a stained white jacket, he bore two iced coffees on a tin tray he balanced over his head. After he had served the drinks, the maître d' dismissed him with an impatient flap of his hand, then turned his obsequious smile back to Joseph.

"*Y ahora*…and now, for your meal, you will have…which?"

Between the old man's imperfect English and Joseph's rudimentary Spanish, their lunch was finally ordered: giant shrimp from the Caribbean coast, boiled whole so that they had to be split and peeled in order to be eaten; a salad of kiwis, mangoes, bananas and pineapple decorated with fuchsia bougainvillea petals; a stone crock filled with fresh, warm tortillas.

Eating shrimp was a total experience, Joseph decided, especially the way Angie did it.

She dispensed with the shells with quick, efficient fingers that denoted a lifetime of living on the coast, dipped the sweet shrimp into the spicy cocktail sauce and popped them in her mouth, oblivious of the juice running down her fingers. Then she sucked on her fingertips to get the last delicious drop.

Joseph watched, entranced.

It was the only way to enjoy shrimp, he thought, peeling his own shrimp while the salty brine dripped from his hands. He knew for a fact that *he* had certainly never enjoyed it quite so much!

He had never before considered eating a particularly sensual experience. But as he watched Angie insert the pink shrimp between her lips that were almost the same color, then follow them with her fingers, delicately sucking the tips one at a time, he found himself unable to turn his eyes away.

He felt his body tightening in anticipation as, like a very satisfied cat, she cleaned one salty-sweet finger and then the next—slowly, as though she herself were savoring the unconscious sensuality of the moment.

With an urgency that shocked him, he wanted to enclose those glistening, wet fingertips with his own lips, to taste their salty sweetness. He knew what the juicy brine tasted like, and he could guess what her fingers would taste like, soft and slow between his lips; the longed-for combination made his body suddenly ache with desire.

He wanted more. He wanted to feel her mouth enclosing his own fingers, feel her tongue flicking across his skin, wet with juice and tiny morsels of shrimp...

Feeling the tension in him mounting unmercifully, he tried to arrest it with small talk. "I like a woman with an appetite," he said, smiling at Angie with a teasing expression, but his voice cracked dangerously.

Appetite conjured up other words and other images. It made him wonder if her appetite for other pleasures in life was as honest and as robust. Drawing them out as long as possible, extracting every last ounce of taste and smell and sight and feeling before she let them carry her inexorably forward to completion. Somehow, he was sure that it was.

"In fact," he blundered on, realizing too late that he was only getting himself in deeper, "you have just about everything I like in a woman." And he proceeded to enumerate her assets.

"You can fish," he said, raising one shrimp-flecked thumb.

"You know how to cook." He raised a glistening, wet forefinger.

"You can handle yourself around a bunch of uncouth fishermen"—his second finger went up.

Then remembering the way she brandished the jagged neck of the broken whiskey bottle that night in the galley, he extended his ring finger. "You'd be a good man to have by my side in a barroom fight—"

Angie laughed gaily.

"And..." he finished, raising his little finger, "you're beautiful. I like that in a woman, too."

Angie glanced at him quickly, smiling uncertainly as though wondering if he were still teasing, then as quickly glanced away. Dipping another giant shrimp into the cocktail sauce, Joseph nipped it neatly in half. Then he scooped it through the red sauce again, and held the remaining portion up to Angie's lips. Slowly, no longer laughing, she opened her mouth to take it between her teeth.

"Beautiful," he repeated, his voice thick, as his eyes darkened from pewter to slate. "I like that in a woman."

They felt the hovering presence of the maître d' the entire time they were eating, and when they had finished, he appeared with lemon-scented finger bowls and hot towels. "To eat the shreemps, it ees ... messy business," he volunteered, smiling. "Ees this not true?"

Joseph took care of the check with an American Express card, leaving a tip large enough that the old man's nights would forever be filled with dreams of more rich *turistas norteamericanos*. He hummed cheerfully as he watched the tall *norteamericano* and the beautiful lady who was not his wife walk out of his café.

Still under the influence of the mandolin and the fragrance of the flowers, they left the café and continued wandering through the village.

Twelve hours. It had sounded like forever at the beginning, but it was only a handful of minutes at the other end. Angie had so fallen under the spell of this enchanting city that she was surprised when she felt a chill in the air and realized that the sun was going down.

Joseph stepped out into the street and hailed a taxi. "Cannery Row," he instructed the driver.

Once settled in the cab, Joseph stretched his arm along the back of the seat. "Is there anything we forgot to do today?" he asked.

"Not a thing. It was perfect."

"Good. That's how I wanted it to be. And entertaining. Were you entertained?"

"Completely." She smiled at him from the opposite side of the back seat. "I hate to see it end."

"No reason why it has to." Joseph leaned forward and spoke to the cabbie. "MamaLina's." He turned back to Angie with a satisfied smile. "I don't have to be the first one back on board. I'll probably end up having to round up a few of the crew anyway."

When he slid back on the seat, in a way neither of them could have explained, he was sitting closer to Angie than he had been before. Instead of moving to his own side of the car, he stayed beside her. His thigh nestled against hers with compelling intimacy, and when he extended his arm across the back of the seat, it rested more on her shoulders than on the peeling vinyl.

Angie strove for a nonchalance she didn't feel. She crossed her legs, and the short, white sundress she wore rode halfway up her thighs. Self-consciously she uncrossed them and pulled the fabric down to cover her knees, then tried without much success to fix her attention on the passing scene. The lights of oncoming cars whizzed past. The cabbie stopped at a red light and she noticed a line of people straggling down the block in front of an all-night movie theater.

Finally the taxi jerked to a halt. "One hundred and thirty *colones,* a dollar-fifty American," the driver announced laconically from the front seat. "You want me to wait, *compadre?*"

"No." Joseph fumbled in his pocket and handed the man several crumpled dollar bills. "Keep it," he grunted.

The cabbie looked surprised.

Chapter Thirteen

Even before Angie's eyes adjusted to the dim interior, she could smell it. The atmosphere was ripe with the odors of sweat and whiskey and spilled beer, and stale cigarette smoke hung in layers on the stagnant air.

MamaLina's was typical of waterfront bars all over the world. Here the dominant language seemed to be Spanish; elsewhere it might be French, or English or Tagalog. It didn't matter. If one didn't listen to the words, the sounds were all the same.

It was more than a little bit seedy and, despite its determined gaiety, somehow sad. It was the other side of the gypsy life, and it was rather like the men themselves: brash on the outside, but with loneliness lurking in the secret corners. After a while the cantinas and bars all over the world became indistinguishable from one another, and the gypsies who frequented them didn't know if they were in Puntarenas or Boston or Baghdad. Or care.

Angie saw that several men from the *Sea Witch* had made MamaLina's their last stop before heading back to the boat. Dominic sat in a crowded booth in the rear with a girl on either arm. Taken together, the ages of the two of them didn't add up to his.

Joseph escorted Angie to a small table beside the postage-stamp dance floor. A bored, dark-haired waitress took their order and delivered two foaming glasses of beer.

"I wonder if it bothers Dominic that he has granddaughters the same age as those girls?" Joseph commented sourly.

Angie looked at him with surprise. "You sound awfully cynical," she said. "Is something bothering you?"

His mood seemed to have changed. He scowled fiercely from beneath furrowed brows. "I shouldn't have brought you here. It never looked quite so...*sleazy* before."

He tossed his hat on the table and picked up one of the glasses of beer, throwing half of it down his throat with one jerky motion, as if it were a shot of whiskey and he was drinking it neat.

"It's not sleazy, exactly," Angie corrected him. "It's more cozy, like you can take off your shoes—" she kicked off her sandals beneath the table and massaged one tired ankle with the toes of the other foot "—and your company manners, and just be yourself."

"Joey! My Joey! How long has it been?" From the other side of the room, a deep voice hailed him. An enormously fat *mestiza* rolled across the dance floor with outstretched arms, which she threw effusively around Joseph's neck. "They tell me you are here, but I don't believe them!"

She took his face in both her fleshy hands and kissed his mouth with a resounding smack.

Joseph half rose, but the fat woman pushed him back down. "Oh-ho, none of that here, my Joey! You know we want you boys to feel like home!" She turned to inspect Angie with an appraising feminine eye. "And your friend is . . . ?"

"We've met, MamaLina," Angie said.

MamaLina looked at her intently. "No, I don't . . . Wait, tell me something. . . ."

"This is Angeli de Vasconceles," Joseph offered.

"No, but that is not right. . . . There is something in the face . . . in the chin. . . ."

"I am Angie Reno," Angie told her quietly.

"Of course!" The fat woman struck her forehead melodramatically with one hand. "Long Jack's girl! How could I forget? Ten years it must be by now! You were only a baby, and I, I was much younger, too. And thinner!"

She chortled. "But not much! And here you are, such a fine young lady, and still in the fleet. What is your papa thinking of, letting such a fine young lady work on the tuna boats, eh? And your papa—where *is* that rascal, anyway? For many years I have not seen him. He is too good for MamaLina now?"

"My father is dead, MamaLina."

"Aii-i-yee. Yes, now it comes back to me!" Her bright black eyes brimmed with tears, which were no less sincere for all their theatrical exaggeration. "Such a terrible thing! Why is it always the young ones, eh?" she demanded fiercely of no one in particular. "I remember your papa—always a laugh on his face, always money in his pockets."

She sniffled and heaved a doleful sigh, then wiped the tears away with fleshy fingers. "Aii-i-yee, that Long Jack!" She chuckled fondly. "Bringing a child on a trip like that! Why is it always the good ones, eh?"

"You've been in business that long, MamaLina?" Joseph broke in, tactfully changing the subject. "I didn't know you were that old!"

"Hah!" she shouted with a coarse and hearty laugh. "I was dishing up my *caldo verde* when you were still too young to eat it!" Still laughing, she slapped her palms on the table and heaved her bulk out of the chair, returning to her station at the end of the bar, from which she could keep a savvy eye on the evening's business.

Angie smiled at Joseph. "I felt like a real fisherman there for a minute. A real gypsy, Cappy would say."

"You *are* a real fisherman. You've been doing awfully well. I have to admit, I never expected it."

"Why not?" When he didn't reply, she persisted curiously. "Why did you hire me in the first place, if you didn't think I'd work out?"

"Doesn't matter now. What I'm wondering is whether it's working out from *your* point of view. Are you laying to rest the ghosts you wanted to?"

"Asa told you that. I'm sorry. It sounds so selfish, using the *Sea Witch* for my own ends...."

"Not at all. Not all men go to sea because they love it, you know. We all have different reasons."

"What are yours?"

"I asked you first."

"Well then...no," she said honestly. "I don't feel that I understand any more than I did before. Why Cappy went to sea, why he kept going, knowing that at any time it could get the best of him. He loved it, I know that. But he didn't have to risk his life. Sometimes I feel..."

"Feel what?" Joseph prompted gently.

Her voice fell. *"... that he loved it more than he loved me,"* she whispered reluctantly. Spoken out loud, it sounded childish even to her own ears, and she was embarrassed.

Joseph considered her last words carefully. "You still see Long Jack the way you did when you were a kid," he said finally. "Larger than life. And Long Jack fit the bill better than most. He *was* larger than life; but he wasn't immortal, and that's what you expected him to be. He was bound to disappoint you."

"You told me that you sailed under him once."

"Yes. Years ago. I was just a greenhorn apprentice, but I never forgot him. He wasn't the kind you forget."

This obscure link between the two men from nearly half a lifetime ago fascinated Angie. "How did it happen that you signed on with him?"

"I needed a summer job. He had one."

"As simple as that?"

"Is anything ever?" Joseph replied, smiling. "No. My father was a lobsterman off the coast of Maine. Never made much money. Then one day he didn't come back, and we were left with nothing, my mother and my younger brother and I. So I quit school and went to work. I was fifteen years old. Long Jack took me on, no questions asked. Treated me like a man, and what I needed most at that time in my life was someone to believe in me.

"We went south that year, through the Panama Canal and then up to Dago. He gave me plane fare home, but I sent it to my mother along with my share and stayed in California."

"You quit school at fifteen?" Angie said. "Dominic told me you got your Master's Papers right out of college."

"That's a good joke on Dominic," he said with gentle irony, as if it were a good joke on himself as well. "No, I never went to college. I never even finished high school. But I've had a good education. The best—experience. And anything I wanted to know, I went to the library and got books about it. Whenever I went to sea, I took along stacks of books. On one trip I read the entire *Encyclopaedia Britannica.*"

It wasn't such an unusual story, except for the reading part. Mano's story was similar. As a matter of fact, so was Cappy's. What *was* unusual was the polish Joseph had acquired along with the experience and the books. He hadn't been *born* smooth, Angie realized suddenly; he had been *worn* smooth. She looked at him with something resembling awe.

Joseph picked up his glass and downed what was left of his beer, then signaled the hovering waitress for another.

"On the house," the girl said when she returned with two more foaming glasses. She ignored the change he pushed toward her. "MamaLina says your money's no good here."

"You take it, then," Joseph suggested. She scooped up the coins and slipped them into the front of her blouse.

Joseph turned his attention back to Angie. "Shall I tell you what it's like, being at sea?"

She demurred. "I've been to sea a few times. I know something about it."

He smiled affably. "I mean *really* being at sea?"

Angie nodded, curious.

"It's hot. Or it's cold. But it's always too much of whatever it is." His voice was hypnotic, and she found herself listening not only to the words, but the strange, pensive inflection behind them.

"The salt gets into your pores and the creases in your skin, and it rubs you raw. You never get the smell of diesel fuel out of your nostrils—the stink of it goes clear to the bone. All the foreign ports you're so anxious to see? No one wants you there, except the pimps, and the girls are diseased anyway. See, these are things your father wouldn't have told you."

He paused. "Ever been out in a storm? A *real* storm?"

Angie shook her head. "A few little squalls, that's all. Nothing, you know, *dangerous* or anything."

"Well, it's like…hell breaking loose all around you, only worse. The wind knocks you around like you're nothing more than a matchstick, and it's whistling past your ears so hard that you can't hear anything else. Your hands are frozen inside your gloves. Sometimes the rain freezes on your eyelashes, and then you can't even close your eyes.

"And you begin to see things in the cloud banks. Ghosts, and ghost ships that went down maybe centuries ago. And they call you. They moan. And if it lasts long enough you begin to doubt what's real and what isn't. Then it's the devil himself you hear, and maybe you even welcome him, because then at least it would be over."

Cigarette smoke hung in still layers on the air—like blue haze, like cloud banks, like the world covered in thick gray gauze. After a minute Joseph looked up and grinned roguishly, dispelling the cloud banks and the ghosts. "You see? It's a rough world, Angie. Long Jack would be the first to tell you that."

"You sound as though you hate it."

"I love it. But I harbor no illusions. I know how...*unforgiving* it can be of even the smallest mistake."

Angie was still for a moment, then spoke in a low, reluctant whisper. "Do you...do you think that my father made...a mistake?" she asked.

"No!" His denial was immediate and emphatic. "No one can say that! Maybe he shouldn't have been out so late in the year, but which of us hasn't taken a few risks when the season's been bad? Still, Long Jack could have gotten them out, if anyone could. He was a brave man—they were all brave men. I think we have to leave it at that."

He was as high-tech as the superseiner he commanded, Angie reflected, yet as full of an old seaman's yarns as Dominic. What he needed, she decided, was a boat of his own, where the risks were his own, and so were the profits. And that's what Reno's could offer him....

Speculatively, her glance perused him, traveling up the long body slouched low in the chair. She was estimating his suitability for the position, she told herself.

She began with his feet, extended under the table and crossed at the ankles, up the long legs to the narrow hips resting precariously on the very edge of his chair, and from there to the arms folded casually over a broad and muscular chest.

She worked her way up to the fascinating indentation of the scarlike cleft in his chin and the dark slash of his mouth, a cigarette hanging loosely from the corner and the lips twisted into a crooked half smile.

When she reached the eyes her inventory stopped, for she saw that he was watching her with the same frank speculation. His smile tightened, as though he'd read her mind and recognized what he'd seen there. He cocked one eyebrow quizzically.

"Dance?" he asked.

Beneath a tarnished glitter ball that caught the light and refracted it downward in a thousand tiny pinpoints, Joseph drew her into the circle of his arms.

The glittering ball rotated in the ceiling, and as it did, its light caught the chain that hung around Joseph's neck and made it sparkle. The golden crucifix reached just below his collarbone, almost hidden in the dark hair of his chest. What had Dominic said? *I bet even a skipper like this one, what got his papers right outta college, bet he's got a bit o' gold on 'im somewheres, too.*

"Why do you wear this?" she asked, touching the golden cross with two fingers.

Joseph covered her fingers with his own. "You know the story of Davy Jones's locker, don't you?" In order to make himself heard above the jukebox, he bent his head and spoke directly into her ear. "Well, I don't believe it's Davy Jones at all. I think it's some kind of sea goddess, myself—and I think she's a mercenary lady! No *man* would ever make another man pay for a little peace of mind the way that lady does!"

"Funny," Angie said, tilting her head back to look up at him. "I wouldn't have thought you were the superstitious type."

"I'm not. But there's this fellow, this sailor I think I used to be in another life—*he's* the one who wears this. He doesn't like to take chances."

"And who was he, this sailor you think you used to be?"

"Oh, he was a lot of things. Maybe he was a galley slave on an old Roman ship. He was a pirate once, I think. I get the feeling he may have been lost at sea many times—that's why he's so careful now. But one thing I know for sure—he's never been able to break the chains that bind him to the sea."

The record on the jukebox changed, becoming a sultry Brazilian love song. The tinny ballad wove a fragile spell—steel guitars carrying the melody, while the incessant rhythm of drums provided a throbbing, pulsating counterpoint. The shabbiness of the cantina was lost in the sensual beat. All the hard edges softened—the scarred dance floor and the cheap wooden tables that surrounded it, the tawdry paint on tired faces, MamaLina's shrewd eyes at the end of the bar, estimating her percent of every *colone* that changed hands.

Even the stained walls faded, becoming a soft cocoon that kept the rest of the world at bay. The only reality was the few feet of wooden floor where Joseph's body was making its first, tentative advances, and Angie's was responding in kind.

Joseph leaned over her, his cheek pressed against her temple, and she could feel his hard body along the full length of hers. She felt defenseless, yet felt no need for defenses, as she had that night in the galley, when he had swept her into his arms and transported her to the safe harbor of his cabin.

With a will of their own, Angie's arms reached up and encircled his neck. She was very aware of her breasts, the way they flattened against his chest, aching to be—what? Freed? Touched? Both, and everything in between. Involuntarily her arms tightened.

"Reno..." Joseph began, lifting his head to look at her. The small muscles at the corners of his mouth tightened it into a thin, strained line. "I think this may have been a mistake...."

Angie glanced up at him with a look that was both shy and instinctively seductive, then lowered her eyes again. Her dark lashes created darker shadows on her olive cheeks. "I don't think so," she replied faintly.

How could it be a mistake, when her body yearned toward his as toward completion? When the firm pressure of his hand at the small of her back anchored her to him with compelling intimacy? And if it was a mistake, she suddenly realized that she didn't want to know. Didn't care.

"The timing is all wrong," Joseph continued as if she hadn't spoken. "And so is the place. And I am—"

"I know. You're the skipper. It's all right. It doesn't matter. To me, it's enough, just feeling this way. I used to wonder if..."

Against his own better judgment he tilted her chin upward with one forefinger. "If... what?"

Unnoticed, the song ended and was replaced by the nasal whine of Garth Brooks. Several couples made their way to the dance floor. The noise of the cantina rose another few decibels and Angie's reply was lost in the hubbub.

The muggy air seemed to have gotten a good deal warmer. Angie felt light-headed, as though she'd been walking in the sun too long, and she noticed fine beads of sweat along Joseph's upper lip. With both hands she pushed her hair back from her face.

"Whew, MamaLina could sure use some air-conditioning," she observed distractedly.

Joseph bent closer and cupped his hand to his ear.

She raised her voice. "MamaLina could use..." But the small talk paled with his proximity. "It's hot," she said simply into his cupped palm.

He grasped Angie's elbow and steered her toward the swinging doors, stopping by their table just long enough to collect her bag and throw his hat and linen jacket over his arm. "We can fix that," he said.

Chapter Fourteen

The noise of the cantina followed them outside, muted only a little by the pounding of breakers on the beach and the sporadic screams of a fretful night bird. The sultry air, scented with cannery fumes and brine and night-blooming jasmine instead of cigarette smoke and stale beer, was only marginally cooler.

Joseph stood silently in the shadows beneath the overhanging tin roof. Lighting a cigarette behind his cupped hand, he held it between thumb and forefinger á la Bogart as he propped himself backward against the wall and watched Angie through eyes kept carefully hooded.

She walked to the edge of MamaLina's wide veranda and lifted the heavy hair off the back of her neck. The full moon made the thin cotton of her dress as transparent as cellophane. It spotlighted the high thrust of her breasts, the smooth inward curve of her waist, the rising swell of full, sensual hips and round, firm thighs.

An Amazon, Joseph said to himself. And all woman—enough for any man. Unbidden, a picture flashed into his mind of the way she had looked that night in the galley, of that magnificent body that he had steadfastly refused to allow himself to even imagine until another man had forced him to look at it.

The sudden ache in his groin angered him. There were women about whom he would have a right to think what he was thinking; this was not one of them. She was under his protection, just like any other member of his crew. Maybe more so, because she was more vulnerable. Obviously she didn't seem to recognize that fact, but he did. He'd known it all along, and had been willing to take the chance to get what he wanted. Reno's.

He'd figured he could handle any problems that might come up.

He'd figured wrong. He'd underestimated her ability as a seaman, and that had been his first mistake.

He'd figured wrong about the crew, too. The scuttlebutt on the boat told Joseph that she had won over even the saltiest advocates of the old ways. The men admired her guts and her no-quarter-asked-or-given attitude; that admiration, Joseph knew, combined with the affection they already felt for Reno's, could very well translate itself into a willingness to give her the chance she needed to put the fishery back on its feet.

But most of all he'd figured wrong about himself. His first automatic response, when she had unwittingly hurled that lush body against him in Asa's office, had been lust, cheerful and uncomplicated. But he knew he could handle that—he always had. If he hadn't believed that, he would never have taken her on.

Now things had changed. The desire was still there, but it was no longer uncomplicated. It had become hopelessly entangled with his responsibilities as skipper and his honor as a man, and even further complicated by the unavoidable fact of his own duplicity.

Now he wanted nothing more than to lock her away in the luxury of his own quarters and keep her there until they got back to Dago, safe from the real and imagined dangers which, through his own stupidity, threatened her: the primitive environment; the demanding routine that made her fall asleep in her chair while the rowdy poker game went on around her; men like Sax.

Men like himself.

Still holding her hair piled on top of her head, Angie turned to look at Joseph over her shoulder. The movement brought the heavy curve of one breast into sharp profile, causing him to bite his lip to keep from groaning out loud.

"Why don't you come out here?" she said. "There's a nice breeze." She was still under the spell of the music and the dancing. Her eyes had a dreamy expression that made Joseph think of bedrooms. The ache in his groin increased.

"I like to look at you" was all he said.

Angie smiled. "I'm glad." Her arms still reached upward, holding her hair up off her neck, and it spilled through her fingers like a length of lustrous silk. The moonlight behind her outlined the womanly silhouette of her body as clearly as if she were wearing nothing at all. "I'm glad you like the way I look. I've always felt I was too...oh, I don't know...too *big*...or something."

"Too big?" Joseph flicked his cigarette over the veranda and was beside her in an instant. He placed a hand on either side of her face and traced with his thumbs the soft line of her mouth. He was acutely aware that he had just lost the battle raging within himself. "How could you ever think that? Don't you know that you're perfect? Hasn't anyone ever told you that you're exactly the size a woman should be?"

"Not really. I didn't know... I was never sure...."

"That's a shame," he said thickly. "You should always be sure, a woman like you..." His words trailed off as he lowered his lips to hers. His thumbs at the corners of her lips gently nudged her lips apart, and she opened her mouth to the hot wetness of his tongue.

This time she was sure. Her physical response was so urgent, so immediate, that she knew her body had been primed for this for the past twelve hours. Maybe longer. Maybe since that night on the foredeck when he draped his arm around her shoulders and together they had watched the whales. She had rerun that scenario over and over in her mind, imagining the other ways it might have gone. Now she was going to find out.

There was only one coherent thought left in Joseph's mind: *I shouldn't have taken her on....*

He slipped one hand behind her head and wove his fingers in her hair. The other hand slid farther down to capture the longed-for fullness of her breast. He could feel the warmth and the dampness, and the quivering anticipation as his fingers took possession first of the firm flesh, then of the tender peak that trembled for his touch. He pinched it between thumb and forefinger, exulting in its exquisite texture and its instinctive, immediate response.

When Angie's breath became nothing more than a low, shuddering moan, when Joseph felt her body begin to writhe against his in the ancient, visceral rhythms of love, he dragged his fingers away from her breast and slid them lower, to where the fire burned the hottest. She shifted her legs to accommodate the new direction his hand was taking.

She felt the wooden banister at her back, then she felt Joseph smoothing the fabric of her dress over the top of her thighs.

The moonlight heightened the angularity of his features. If Angie could have seen his face at that moment, she would have seen the face of a *conquistador,* not an honorable one, but one reckless and cruel, prepared to seize a woman of the enemy and show her the power of that strange, foreign place from which he came. Duty was lost in the surging tide that swept over him. As was honor.

"I knew you'd be like this," he whispered hoarsely. "All those nights when I couldn't sleep, knowing you were so close I could almost reach out and touch you, I knew you'd be like this...."

Suddenly the saloon doors burst open, and a trio of boisterous sailors stumbled out. They were very drunk. Their uniforms, apparently once summer whites, were rumpled and stained, and they were cursing loudly and good-naturedly in slurred Cockney slang. Britishers.

Quickly Joseph pulled Angie back in to the shadows, holding her motionless until the sailors had staggered down the rickety steps and into the deserted street. When they had disappeared into another cantina, he loosened his grip. Stepping out of the shadows, he walked to the edge of the veranda and pulled another cigarette from the crumpled pack in his pocket, which he lit with a hand that shook.

It was the galley all over again. It was Sax. He swore under his breath. He would have killed the man for even a hint of what had been in his own mind tonight. He wondered if Angie suspected how tenuous had been the leash on his self-control? He wondered if she had suspected the violence of which he knew he was also capable, the hot masculine aggression that made him want her in the same way Sax had. Quickly. With or without her consent.

He raised his eyes toward the spongy tropical sky and sucked raggedly on the cigarette, then expelled the smoke in a series of explosive puffs. "I *knew* this was a mistake," he said roughly.

Angie walked up behind him. She slipped her arms around his waist and pressed her cheek to his back. Her fingers slipped between the buttons of his shirt to move sensuously through the mat of hair on his chest. "It couldn't be, not the way I feel."

"What could you possibly feel toward me?" he replied, voice rougher still, taking another deep drag on his cigarette. "You don't know anything about me."

"I know what I need to know. And I also know that I haven't felt like this since ... since ..."

"Your husband?" Everything else he'd figured about her had proven to be wrong, but somehow he knew before he said it that he had hit the mark with this one. He felt her cheek rub against his shoulder blade as she nodded.

"Please," she continued almost inaudibly. "I used to wonder if I'd ever...feel this way again. I don't want to lose it now."

Joseph dropped his cigarette to the veranda and ground it out with the toe of one foot. Then turning, he clasped Angie's bare upper arms in his big hands and pulled her gently against his chest. "You won't lose it. I promise you that. *We* won't lose it."

He kissed her, a chaste, closed-mouth kiss, as solemn as a vow. "This isn't the time or the place. But there'll be another time." *I promise you that, too,* he assured his wildly remonstrating body, where the punishing ache was only beginning to subside. "And it'll be right."

The disappointment in her eyes sent a tingle through him that brought the ache back in spades. "Besides," he added with a ghost of a smile, "correct me if I'm wrong, but I'd guess that you're not . . . *protected.*"

"Well, actually, no," Angie replied, returning his smile ruefully. "But I thought *you* would be. You know all those rumors I keep hearing about sailors having a girl in every port . . . ?"

Joseph had the grace to look sheepish. "Look, Angie, I'm not an inexperienced guy. . . ."

"Of course not," she teased solemnly.

"I've been divorced a long time. There was never any reason not to . . ."

"Of course not."

He kissed her once more, then dropped his arm around her shoulders and escorted her down the rickety stairs. "But, no," he said with a wry chuckle. "As a matter of fact, I wasn't prepared, either."

Although, in a way, he *had* been prepared. He hadn't known that this would happen. He refused to admit even to himself how much he wanted it to happen. But he *did* have to acknowledge that he'd briefly fingered one of the little foil packets in his top bureau drawer, and then for reasons only dimly articulated in his own mind, made a deliberate decision to leave it there.

It had something to do with his position as skipper and Angie's as crew. But it had more to do with the pledge he'd made to himself when he signed her on—that his intentions were strictly honorable.

It was a pledge he meant to keep. Never mind that pain throbbed low in his gut like that of a teenager petting in the back seat of his daddy's car. He had done the right thing. The only thing.

And he wondered, not for the first time in his life, why the right thing sometimes felt so damned wrong?

"ALL PRESENT or accounted for," reported the young fisherman on watch when he saw the skipper come across the gangplank with Reno. He handed the duty roster to Joseph. "The new driver came aboard at 2400 hours."

"Thanks, Rodrigues." Joseph quickly scanned the roster and handed it back to the watch. "See you get some shut-eye when your relief comes on." He glanced up at the boy and grinned. "You look like you had a good time on the beach."

"Yessir! I did, sir." Rodrigues tried to look penitent and failed miserably.

"You'd better get some sleep, too, Reno," Joseph said as he turned toward Angie, his voice curt and "skipperlike" in deference to Rodrigues's presence. "You have to get up in a couple of hours."

Still maintaining a discreet distance for Rodrigues's benefit, Joseph and Angie walked aft. Their own long shadows preceded them on the moonlight-washed deck. When they were out of Rodrigues's line of vision, Joseph caught her around the waist, bringing her to an abrupt standstill. Slowly she twirled around, her arms already reaching for him. He leaned backward against the bulkhead and pulled her into the V of his widespread legs, taking possession of her mouth with a purposeful thoroughness. He knew this was going to have to last him for a very long time.

One of his arms was a steel bar behind Angie's neck, the other more steel at the small of her back. Crushed against him from breast to belly, she felt the dimension of his passion caged within the confines of his trousers. Her body instinctively undulated toward it with a slow and impossibly exquisite tightening of her hips.

He lifted her to her toes, and his deliberate mouth moved down the exposed white column of her throat.

Angie swallowed convulsively, then threw her head back to allow his lips greater access. Her unseeing eyes strayed into the dark corridor behind them. Suddenly she stiffened.

"Joseph," she breathed. Her voice came out a panic-stricken hiss. "Joseph!" she tried again, more loudly this time. "Let me go!" She struggled to free herself from his grasp. "Something's wrong! I think there's... there's someone in the galley!"

It took less than a heartbeat for her alarm to transmit itself to him. He released her instantly, shoving her none-too-gently against the wall.

"Where?" he demanded. Shielding her with his body, his eyes darted swiftly over the moon shadows on the deck and into the dark interior of the corridor.

"There!" She pointed toward the galley hatch. The door hung at a crazy angle, a thin crack of light showing along the edge.

"It looks...*broken*," she added in a uncertain voice as she peered over the barrier of his shoulder.

"The pins have been taken out of the hinges," Joseph concurred grimly.

Suddenly Angie noticed wisps of smoke seeping out through the narrow opening. She gasped and took a step closer. Joseph immediately barred her path. Unable to see inside because of the boards nailed where the window used to be, he moved into the corridor and put his ear to the door. Hearing nothing, he pushed the crooked door open.

The light came from the open refrigerator door.

"What the . . . ?" The galley reeked with the nauseating odor of burnt rubber. Joseph held one hand to his nose and slammed the other against the light switch on the wall.

Angie gasped.

All the food lockers hung open and their contents spilled out onto the floor. Plates, cookware and silverware were strewn everywhere, liberally coated with flour, sugar and cereal from the huge sacks split open in the storeroom. Everything was glued together by dozens of eggs smashed against the bulkheads and floor, already beginning to harden around the edges.

The sickening smell of burning rubber came from a metal trash can that smoldered in the middle of the room. Joseph tore off his linen blazer. Using it to protect his hands, he seized the smoldering trash can and carried it outside, where he lifted it into the air and hurled it overboard. It fell into the water with a sickening sizzle. Angie grabbed a dishtowel to hold over her nose as she raced across the galley and flung open the porthole.

"Sax," Angie breathed.

"Rodrigues!" Joseph bellowed.

The watch came running. His jaw dropped in astonishment when he saw the mess. "Jeez, Skipper, what happened?"

"I was hoping you could tell me," Joseph said grimly.

"Jeez, Skipper, I didn't hear anything. Honest!"

Angie interrupted. "He's right. Look, nothing's broken, nothing's smashed. Whoever did it must've been very careful not to make any noise."

"Who'd you relieve?" Joseph asked Rodrigues.

"Dominic."

"He said nothing?"

"No sir!" Rodrigues stared at the ruined galley, obviously impressed by the extent of the damage. "Jeez, Skipper, what a mess!"

"Carry on." Joseph dismissed him, and Rodrigues, still gaping in awe, backed out of the door.

"Sax," Angie said again.

"Sure. I should have expected something like this. He's miles away by now, of course—probably knows his way around the rat's maze of a city better than anyone. We'll never find him."

Joseph looked around the galley. His face was as dark as the black smoke that hung in the putrid air. "What in hell *is* that god-awful smell, anyway?" he muttered to himself. "*Burnt rubber?* Where in hell did he get rubber?"

Angie made her way around the devastation, careful not to touch the slimy, sticky bulkheads, and peered into her tiny cabin. It was then that she realized how thorough Sax had been.

Her clothes were missing from the hooks on the wall. The sheets from her bunk were also missing. There was no trace of her small stash of novels, nor of the meager cache of personal items she kept in a seabag beside the bunk. The room reeked of whiskey, and she realized that her mattress had been liberally doused with the contents of the liquor locker.

She turned in the doorway and slumped against the jamb. "That burned rubber was my seaboots," she informed Joseph dolefully. "And everything else I had in the world!"

In Joseph's eyes she saw a wrath that surpassed her own. Her personal space had been viciously ravaged, and she felt angry and violated. But Joseph's authority had been insulted. To a man whose word on the high seas was as absolute as God's, Angie knew that indignity was far worse than the damage to the boat. Several emotions, all of them intimidating, flickered across his face.

She shivered. Suddenly she was very, very glad that Sax had not stayed around to gloat.

"You're going to need to reorder," Joseph said, in a brusque voice that fought for self-control and achieved it.

"Yes."

"And you're going to need something to wear...."

"Yes."

"I'll put off sailing until 0900 hours. Take the launch later over to the commissary at Hangman's Landing. And take a few of the men along to give you a hand— we don't have any time to waste."

Angie nodded, then cast a dubious eye over the chaos that surrounded them. "I'd better get busy," she said with a sinking heart. From freewheeling gypsy to household drudge in twelve short hours, she told herself glumly. Welcome back to reality!

Without a word Joseph went into the trashed storeroom and came out with a utility broom, a mop and a bucket. He tossed the broom across the room to Angie. "*We'd* better get busy," he corrected. "It's going to be morning soon."

She saw that he was caught in the grip of a fury greater than she could comprehend. She also saw that

he was able to compartmentalize that fury, put it completely out of his mind until a more appropriate time
to deal with it.

His willpower, she marveled, was astonishing. But
then, hadn't she already learned that, back on
MamaLina's old wooden veranda?

Chapter Fifteen

It was a far cry from the stainless-steel laboratory it had been when the trip began, Angie thought, surveying her ruined galley while she assembled a quick lunch for Dominic.

The eggs had made runny streaks down the bulk-heads that no amount of scrubbing could erase; they would have to be repainted when the *Sea Witch* reached San Diego. The window on the galley hatch was still boarded up, since replacing the glass, too, would have to wait for San Diego.

What daylight there was came through the salt-pitted porthole over the sink, which Angie kept open in all but the wettest weather to neutralize the stink of whiskey that had soaked into the floorboards.

Dominic, however, eyes at half-mast, didn't even notice the bizarre decor. He had stumbled into the galley for a quick pick-me-up cup of scalding black coffee, and Angie had insisted that he needed something more than caffeine to fuel his exhausted body.

Sitting at the table with his head propped in one hand, he looked as though he hadn't slept since the boat had left Puntarenas. Which in fact, he hadn't. None of the men had, but no one minded, because the unscheduled stop proved to have been a turning point of sorts in a season plagued by misfortune.

Before Puntarenas, the *Sea Witch* was a laughing-stock. Joseph was well aware that his boat had become the butt of jokes that would be told and repeated all up and down the sea lanes, south to Panama and north past Baja and Dago clear up to Seattle. And it galled him.

First there had been the defection of old Tio Leo, and his Panamanian replacement who couldn't stay out of the cooking sherry; then there was the damaged diesel that forced a return to San Diego. There was also the sailing with a woman on board, always a bad omen. And finally there was the sudden, unexplained jaunt to Puntarenas, which his counterparts on other boats were derisively eager to interpret as a pleasure trip.

In every port where tuna boats called, Joseph knew that references to the *Sea Witch* would be colored with thinly veiled innuendos as to the eyesight and manhood of her crew, and their inability to find fish in a barrel.

But with their return to the fishing grounds after Puntarenas, all that changed. Suddenly the fishermen couldn't haul the fish in fast enough. Joseph had found fish that "had no tails"—meaning they didn't bolt or go deep. They just swam around in neat, orderly and vast schools, fairly begging to be caught.

Joseph worked his men hard, but no harder than he worked himself. At the end of their eighteen-hour days, the crew no longer sat around the galley table playing poker. Instead they fell into their bunks in sleep so heavy, it seemed drugged, waking only to stand their watches until there was daylight enough to begin fishing again.

For the *suerte*—the luck—to turn around like this was the kind of occurrence from which legends were born. Years later, on other boats in other oceans, men would gather as they always did in the evenings, in the galley or on the foredeck, and someone would tell the story, with all the obligatory embellishments, of *this* boat, and *this* season, and *this* skipper.

"THE MEN ARE GETTING tired," Angie observed to Dominic, watching him wolf his *chorizo* and beans. "They're running on pure nerve—pretty soon they're going to start making mistakes."

Dominic disagreed. He looked at her patronizingly through bleary, red-rimmed eyes, while his hand clamped his mug of coffee as if its caffeine were a lifeline.

"Ye dont understand, Angie girl," he said almost cheerfully. "Man waits a lifetime for a season like this. Long's the fish hold out, we will. I remember another trip like this one. With Old Jack, yer grandfather, it was, off the coast o' Africa. We was jest lads then...." He ran out of steam. "Well, he must'a told ye. Man dont fergit a thing like that."

Dominic looked every day of his sixty-odd years, Angie thought compassionately. As deckboss, his constant presence was required on deck during the off-loading of the catch, but he didn't look as though he had many more sets left in his stooped, sunburned old body.

He was Montero's employee, of course; but if he were hers, she'd...what? Retire him? And take away his self-respect? Or let him kill himself trying to do a younger man's job? Being an owner, Angie was beginning to realize, was going to bring its own unique set of problems.

Cadaverous-faced Madruga plodded into the galley. He looked only marginally less fatigued than Dominic. "Reno, Skipper says will you bring him up a tray?" Like any request from the skipper, it was not of course a question.

Dominic dragged his stiff body to its feet.

"Sit, sit, old man," Madruga said tiredly. He clapped Dominic on the shoulder and pushed him back into the chair. "Skipper says we're gonna sit this one out."

Balancing a loaded tray on one hand, Angie climbed the ladder to the speedboat deck and walked forward to the bridge. Regretfully she glanced down at her jeans-and-chambray-shirt uniform.

In her determination to overcome the handicap of femininity, she had not brought even a lipstick aboard the *Sea Witch*, nor a single pair of the tiniest, most unobtrusive earrings to adorn the empty holes in her earlobes. She knew that her hair frizzed in dark, unruly curls around her face. If her eyes were heavy-lidded, it was not from mascara but from lack of sleep, and if there was a touch of color in her cheeks, it was only from the heat of the cookstove.

Now, when she wanted so much to remind Joseph of the woman she had been that night in Puntarenas, she was afraid that she was more than ever a far cry from Cappy's fond comparison to Helen of Troy.

Taking a deep breath, she opened the door of the bridge and stepped inside. Joseph was in the chart room, logging tonnage into the boat's computer.

He glanced up with a quick, preoccupied smile. "Angie. Thanks. Just put it down anywhere." Then he returned his attention to the computer, continuing to pore over the information he was recording.

Angie, who had not had a private word with him since the night they had worked side by side until dawn in the vandalized galley, seized this opportunity to slip into a chair and watch him work.

With the frenzied, round-the-clock fishing that had been taking place for the past week, she had hardly had time to remember everything that had happened at Puntarenas. It seemed like a very long time ago. That desirable, desirous woman at MamaLina's seemed like someone *else*—someone whose hands weren't nicked by paring knives and potato peelers and roughened by dishwater, whose muscles didn't ache, whose eyes weren't heavy with fatigue.

Did he remember, she wondered, in those brief snatches of time he had to himself while he was on the radio in the crow's nest? While he paced the deck, a cigarette bobbing furiously in the corner of his mouth as he barked orders to his crew? In those moments at night before he fell into an exhausted sleep?

Beneath the ruddy tan, his face had the pallor of strain—too much coffee, too little sleep, too little food gulped much too quickly.

"You look tired," Angie said softly.

Joseph looked up, and his face was as drawn as Dominic's. "So do you." He rolled his big shoulders backward and forward. He stretched his back with a long and satisfying groan. He fixed his weary eyes on the restful blue water beyond the bow. Then he clasped his hands behind his head, leaned back in his chair, and grinned broadly. "Fantastic run of luck, isn't it?"

"You'd better thank Buengiovanni for that."

Joseph eyed her quizzically. "Buengiovanni?"

"He performed some sort of ritual he said would lift the curse—the *praga,* he called it—from the boat. I know because he got the eggs from me."

"*Eggs?*"

Angie smiled. "He was a little embarrassed about it, but he said it couldn't hurt."

"What was this...*ritual?*"

"Well, he rolled about two dozen eggs through some spices he burned in a coffee can—fresh spices would be better, he said, but he'd use what was at hand. Then he went around hiding them in all those little, out-of-the-way places where the evil *bruxos* stow themselves."

"Any of the other men know about this?"

"They all did."

Joseph snorted ironically. "Amazing, isn't it? They go to sea on a modern, state-of-the-art ship, and then they hide eggs in corners to get rid of evil spirits!" He threw back his head and laughed. "You see why I love this job!"

"I only hope we can find the whole two dozen by the time we get back to San Diego," Angie retorted dryly, "Or we're *really* going to have *bruxos* aboard this boat!"

Reluctantly she got to her feet. "I'd better get back. Your lunch is getting cold."

"No, don't go. I've decided to take a break this afternoon, anyway.

"I *will* thank Buengiovanni," he said. "Who knows whether it's my consummate skill as a skipper or his in driving out the *bruxos?* Who can say what works?"

"Does that sailor you used to be believe in *bruxos?*" Angie asked with a smile. "Because I'm pretty sure *you* don't. I'd be willing to bet Buengiovanni doesn't, either!"

"Ah, but you're wrong. *Bruxos* are everywhere. We may *call* them something else—waterspouts, riptides, currents that tangle up the nets so that we lose a whole day repairing them—but that's what they are."

His gray eyes narrowed to slanted lines above his cheekbones as he gave Angie a teasing grin. "Me, for instance. There were *bruxos* in me the day I told Asa Cox to hire you. Oh yes, *bruxos!* I thought I took you on for my own reasons, and now I find that the *bruxos* had reasons of their own. They're probably laughing at me from all those hidey-holes where they stow away!"

"Does that mean you're sorry?"

"Sorry?" He drummed his fingers on the arm of his chair, appearing to consider the question seriously. "I don't know about that. It *does* mean that there's not a minute of the day when you're not on my mind. It means that I drive myself until I'm so tired I can identify each muscle in my body by its own, separate ache, and the minute my head hits the pillow, there you are. It means . . ."

His eyes narrowed; they looked as though they were closed. He saw her the way she appeared every night in his dreams, framed in steamy tropical moonlight—the intoxicating, hourglass sculpture of her body, outlined all around by nothing more substantial than a gauzy web of white cotton.

His face looked sheepish, and there was a suggestive edge to his voice that he couldn't quite disguise. "It means that if I could have back that one night in Puntarenas, I think I'd do things differently this time!"

Chapter Sixteen

The men were edgy. They glanced far too often out the galley porthole between hands of their endless poker game. Enormous amounts of money usually changed hands at these games, but on this day the game limped along indifferently while the men gave most of their attention to the weather.

Angie, too, kept one eye on her cards and the other on the open porthole, ready to jump up and close it the moment the rains came.

From where she sat she could see row upon row of flat, stratus clouds scudding across the darkening sky. They piled on top of each other, dense as tuna in a net, until they layered the entire horizon. Through a filter of uncertain sunlight, the blue sky was turning a dull pewter, and the scudding clouds were tinged with a sickly yellow cast.

It was a mackerel sky, the kind of sky that made men uneasy, for it meant change.

"What's the skipper say?" one deckhand asked of no one in particular.

"Aint said nothin' yet," big, blond Tennessee volunteered in his drawl. "There's supposed to be a typhoon blowing up due east, but it aint supposed to come within a couple hundred miles of us."

"Skipper's on the bridge," Pinheiro offered, discarding a two of hearts and an ace. "Seen him there myself, not more'n an hour ago."

"Well, there wasn't anything showing up at noon," Dominic said positively. "Clear as glass at noon."

"You don't need no instruments to tell you a sky like that signifies storm," the deckhand said sourly.

"Fish'er gone," Pinheiro pointed out, not looking up as he drew two cards with methodical concentration.

"Play cards!" demanded one player, who obviously held a winning hand.

Another slapped his cards facedown on the table and got up to refill his coffee cup. "Shoot," he muttered. "I dont like the feel of this. Dont like it one damn bit!"

As though in reply, the boat began to dip on a swell that extended the full length of the horizon. It was a hint, and an ominous one, of some power building up underneath the waves. The cupboard doors clicked against their latches as their contents shifted with each roll.

Angie scraped her chair away from the table. Peering out the porthole, she frowned. The top of the mast had disappeared into the lowering sky. A smear of light remained in the north, but to the south, the sun was lost behind a curtain of lead.

The wind began to howl.

"It's the witch, all right," said one man, and crossed himself.

Joseph's voice crackled over the intercom. "All hands duty stations."

Like bullets from a gun, the men shot out of the galley. Angie found herself alone in a silence so sudden that it was still full of echoes. She reached automatically for the orange life jacket hanging inside the storeroom door, and buckled it around her waist.

Through the porthole, she saw that the whole world was gunmetal now, a solid mass of roiling sea and sky, and impossible to tell where one ended and the other began. Tiny beads of sweat formed at her hairline and on her upper lip.

A bolt of lightning ripped the sky, and then another. The electricity flickered once, twice, and then went out. Immediately the emergency generator took over, illuminating the galley with an eerie white light. With the emergency generator, the halogen searchlights also switched on and began a restless sweeping of the sea-washed decks.

The boat was filled with unfamiliar sounds—mysterious cracks and creaks, forboding groans, unknown feet running topside. Trying to quell her rising panic, Angie concentrated instead on trying to identify them. There were many sounds she couldn't recognize.

And then one that she could.

It was above her on the speedboat deck—a clattering that seemed to begin some distance away, pass directly overhead, then clatter away again. With sinking heart Angie realized what it was; the enormous crane that lowered the speedboats for the chase and picked them up afterward. It must have broken loose from its mooring, and was lurching across the speedboat deck with every roll of the storm-tossed *Sea Witch*.

She listened for the sound of footsteps that would indicate someone else had heard and was on the way.

Nothing. The wind must be carrying the sound away from the engine room, she finally decided. No one else would hear; no one else would be coming.

And if they lost the crane, they lost the season. She knew that.

THE WIND RIPPED the hatch out of Angie's hands. It flapped madly against the bulkhead before she could lean her weight against it and force it closed. Unable to see, she clipped her life jacket to the safety rope attached to the bulkhead and began to feel her way forward. Her yellow oilskin and sou'wester encased her like a rubber sheet from head to knees, and still the rain managed to penetrate clear through to her clammy skin.

Seawater sloshed over the railing. The *Sea Witch* shuddered perilously in the wind. Angie battled for every inch she gained along the treacherous deck, and after what seemed like an eternity, she felt the aluminum ladder in her hand.

Still attached to the bulkhead by the umbilical cord of her safety rope, she started up. Nearly blind and fighting the wind, the climb that normally took a few seconds now cost her several precious minutes.

Once on the speedboat deck, she tried to locate the marauding crane. Her visibility was hampered by the driving rain but suddenly, in a heart-stopping bolt of lightning, she sighted it. Yellow steel with a boom two stories high, it was hurtling headlong through the swirling mist directly toward her. The speedboats that lay in its path were already crushed beyond recognition.

As it made its pass, Angie clutched at the lashing cable. It whipped out of her grasp and sent her sprawling. She felt her boots fill with water. Scrambling to her knees, she could only watch helplessly as the crane, with the next roll of the *Sea Witch*, careened away.

The second time the crane came hurtling, Angie, still on her knees, grabbed at the cable with strength born of desperation. She felt the rope rough and swollen and solid in her hands. Then the *Sea Witch* rolled again, and she knew she wouldn't be able to hold on.

But in the split second before it pulled out of her hand, she felt the cable jerk downward. The flash of another lightning bolt revealed a second pair of gloves on the cable beside hers.

Angie's fingers ached. Her arms felt as though they were being torn from their sockets, but inch by tortuous inch the two pair of hands twisted the cable around the giant cleat that would secure the crane to the deck. Only when she was certain that it would not tear loose again was she able to unclench the fingers that were frozen like claws to the cable.

For a minute Angie remained on her knees, coughing as though she'd just run a marathon. She threw her head back and inhaled huge, painful gulps of air. Finally it occurred to her to wonder who was behind the other pair of hands. She parted the dripping hair the wind and rain had plastered to her face and looked up.

The hands belonged to Joseph. He was livid.

"Are you crazy?" She knew that he must be shouting because she could see clear down to his tonsils, but the shrieking wind carried the words away before they reached her ears. Bracing her hands on her knees, she pushed herself wearily to her feet.

"Get below!" She read his lips while his arms gesticulated in some kind of ferocious pantomime. Behind his shoulder Angie could see Otis's blurred and anxious face gawking at her from the bridge, and the back of Madruga's head as he wrestled with the wheel.

"Get below!" Joseph shouted again, again without a sound.

When Angie jerked her head curtly and started toward the ladder, he turned into the wind and began to make his way laboriously back toward the bridge. His progress was measured in inches.

Angie found the top rung with the toe of one booted foot and began to descend. Suddenly, from seemingly out of nowhere, a thought flashed into her mind: a storm like this...it could have been a storm like this....

What were those stories Joseph had told her, that night at MamaLina's? *It's like hell breaking loose.* His hypnotic words came back to her, insinuating themselves into her imagination like seeds finding fertile ground. *And you begin to see things in the cloud banks. Ghosts and ghost ships that went down maybe centuries ago. And they call you....*

A night like this...what must it have been like, a night like this, four years ago? *You begin to doubt what's real and what isn't....*

Arriving at the bottom of the ladder, Angie caught sight of something through the claustrophobic walls of rain. She paused uncertainly. The rolling mists had gathered themselves into a shape that seemed somehow vaguely familiar. It was hazy, no more solid, really, than the gray mist that surrounded it. It almost looked like a ship, or part of a ship.

A night like this.... She peered closer.

"Cappy?" she whispered, or thought she did, incredulously. "Cappy?" she tried to say more loudly, her heart beginning to pound.

The mists rolled again. "Cappy!" she suddenly cried aloud, but the sound was carried away by the wind, and it was as though she hadn't spoken at all.

He stood in the wheelhouse, motionless. The muscles of his big arms strained with superhuman effort, and his legs were braced like pillars on the thrashing deck. His face was as impassive as stone, but even through the sheets of rain Angie could see the veins standing out like cords in his neck. The knuckles that gripped the wheel were white.

He didn't turn. He didn't even move. He stood as he would stand for all eternity—staring straight ahead, unblinking eyes watching death.

Where the deck would be, she almost imagined she could see Mano and the rest of the crew. They were trying desperately to lower the lifeboats, which the wind caught and tossed away as soon as they were cut loose. Bright orange life jackets glowed like fire in the fading gray light.

"Mano," Angie whispered. Or thought she did. He wasn't lashed to anything, none of them were. It must be too late for that, then; now they were just trying to get free of the boat before it split apart. A wave larger than the others washed over the railing, and when it was gone, several of the orange life jackets went over the side with it. They hung for an heartbreaking moment on the churning surface, then another wave carried them under.

Angie imagined Mano, the way he would have hauled himself to his feet on the perpendicular deck and struggled aft toward the men and the only remaining lifeboat. But as she watched in horror, their last hope somersaulted with a crash against the heaving bulkhead, and was swept into the maelstrom. The faces of the doomed men were granite in the eerie light, a gray granite rough-hewn from the darker gray granite of the sky.

Then, as Angie watched, Long Jack's old *Mackerel Sky,* which had disappeared without a trace four years earlier in a freak North Atlantic hurricane, vanished again, this time slipping noiselessly into the dark troughs of a South Pacific typhoon.

There had been no witnesses to the first tragedy. There were two tonight: the daughter of the captain of the ill-fated vessel and, hidden in the shadow of the bridge, out of reach of the searchlights that swept the deck, the skipper of the tuna boat *Sea Witch.*

Joseph had waited to make sure Angie got safely down the ladder and into the galley. When he saw her steps slow and then come to a halt, when he saw her gaze turn outward into the storm, he suspected that the ghosts she'd come aboard to bury had finally materialized.

He could guess what she was seeing through the wide and haunted eyes that, oblivious of the stinging rain, stared into the nothingness beyond the railing. Oh, not specifically, of course, but close enough. He had a few ghosts of his own that showed up occasionally on the opaque canvas of rain during a blow, or when the fog was thick, or the night particularly dark.

Sometimes he saw the old sailorman he liked to think he had been in another life; sometimes, unknown ships of uncertain origins. Sometimes it was the gaunt, blurred image of a lobsterman, a figure remembered mostly in his dreams, shrouded head to toe in sou'wester, oilskin and seaboots, poling his tiny dory bit by bit into the great, silent maw of a Grand Banks fog, which would never spit him back.

Joseph's eyes were narrowed to mere slits against the fierce raindrops that stung like needles when they struck his skin, and they were riveted on Angie's face. His own face devoid of expression, he watched her watch her father's boat go down, all hands on board.

Chapter Seventeen

"Are you all right?" Joseph's voice came to her as from a great distance. "Answer me!"

The eyes she fixed on him were empty. They seemed to have trouble remembering who he was. He jerked her away from the railing and half pushed, half pulled her in the direction of the galley, where he shoved her inside.

"Are you all right?" he asked again.

Angie nodded dazedly.

"Are you sure?"

Her nod became stronger.

"Okay, then, stay here. Don't go outside, no matter what you hear, understand? I'll be back as soon as I can." He backed out, pulling the hatch shut behind him.

Still disoriented, Angie stumbled to the porthole. She gripped the edge of the counter with stiff fingers and peered out at the storm. Nothing. Nothing but the terrible grayness and the spume that washed over the railing and the rain that crashed against the round pane of glass.

The mists had rolled on, and the ghost ship was gone. Not even a bit of debris or an oil slick left on the surface of the water to mark where she had been. That was what the searchers had all said four years ago; tonight Angie finally, irrevocably understood that it was true.

Uncanny, she thought, the way your mind plays tricks on you when you're tired and cold and wet and miserable. And yet... She frowned, trying to put her finger on something elusive that hovered just beyond her ability to recall.

And yet... In her hallucination, Mano had been wearing a bulky knit sweater she'd never seen before. And his hair was longer than he ever allowed it to grow, shoreside.

Cappy had looked different, too. Gaunt. The lines around his mouth were etched crevice-deep; his eyes were like stones from which no reflection came.

And Long Jack's beloved old *Mackerel Sky*—there was rust on her hull, and she was faded, washed out to the colorless gray of driftwood, as if she'd been beached for a long, long time in the sun....

The *Sea Witch* gave a sickening lurch backward. The precipitous shift threw Angie off-balance, knocking her headlong against the heavy oak table. She hit it with a bone-jarring thud, then turned and clutched its solid edge as though it were a life raft, as though it was the only reality in a world suddenly gone crazy.

Clammy beads of sweat formed on her forehead. *As if she'd been beached for a long, long time in the sun....*

The wind rattled the mast in short, staccato bursts that sounded like the snatches of phrases a radioman might use.... *Mayday. Mayday. We are the* Mackerel Sky *out of San Diego. Mayday. Mayday. We are the*

Makerel Sky out of San Diego. Latitude 45.5°, longitude 57°. We are going down. Repeat...

No distress signals were ever received from the old *Mackerel Sky*. But her radioman had been Sharkey Sims, and Angie knew Sharkey, knew that he would have stayed at his post until the very forces of hell itself ripped him away.

Hours dragged by and the storm raged on. Losing all sense of time, Angie could no longer be sure whether it was day, or night, or even the next day.

This was fear at its most primitive. The absolute power of the sea, its monumental *indifference* to the plight of these few humans and their pitiful shell of fiberglass-and-steel brought terror home to her like a fist to the stomach. Was this the way they felt? she wondered. Cappy? Mano? All the men who'd ever made their livings on the sea? What courage it must have taken!

That they were heros she had always known—rowdy, reckless, swashbuckling adventurers, yes. But the unsung courage of doing battle with the sea like this, year after year, knowing all the while how insignificant they were in the face of that fury—*that* was the real heroism. And that was something she had never truly understood.

Until now.

A wave of humility washed over her. *I didn't know!*

Angie no longer felt like a sailor, or a fisherman or even one of Cappy's gypsies. She was only tired and terrified and confused, and beginning to experience the unfamiliar nausea of seasickness.

Making her way hand over hand to the corner between the cupboards and the food locker, she slid wearily down the bulkhead to the floor. She leaned her head backward against a cupboard door, crossed her arms over the ungainly life jacket around her waist and ordered herself to get some rest. She realized that it was going to be a very long night...day...whatever....

A WHIRLWIND OF RAIN gusted into the galley. Angie's first thought was the terrifying certainty that a main hatchway had given way and the sea was flooding in.

Then through the wind and rain that swirled around the galley like a minitornado, she realized that the thrashing door was being restrained by Joseph, who quickly stepped inside and forced it shut.

"Joseph!" Angie scrambled to her feet. "What are you doing here?"

He dragged the sou'wester from his head and shook the excess water onto the floor. "I thought you might be frightened."

"I'm not afraid. I'm *terrified!* But I can handle it."

"I didn't doubt that for a minute." Joseph dropped the empty thermos he was carrying into the sink, where it clinked restlessly with each roll of the boat. Then he draped himself on one corner of the table and folded his arms across the orange life jacket buckled around his chest, and smiled at Angie reassuringly.

"Where did this weather come from?" she asked, trying to keep a tremor of fear out of her voice, and unexpectedly finding it not so difficult now that Joseph was near.

"Typhoon," he replied. "It was off Costa Rica yesterday. Then it changed course and came north. Actually, it's not such a bad blow, and we're only getting the tail end of it."

Leaning backward against the counter on outspread arms, Angie eyed him skeptically, plainly unconvinced. The heels of her palms braced for dear life on the slick Formica surface. Her feet were planted apart, knees slightly bent so that she could shift her weight from one foot to the other to maintain her balance on the pitching floor.

She looked as tough and indefatigable as any other member of the crew, Joseph observed with a chivalrous stab at impartiality. But there was a touching vulnerability around the wide eyes filled with false bravado and around her tremulous mouth that served to enhance her earthy femininity by trying so ineffectually to disguise it.

On this storm-tossed night, when earth itself seemed farther away than the tides of eternity, he found that earthy sensuality irresistible. Besides, the raging elements were a powerful aphrodisiac, appealing to other primal forces within him, just as elemental and just as powerful.

"Hey, this isn't so bad!" he exclaimed heartily, trying with limited success to overcome the compelling hunger in his voice. "I've seen worse. We all have."

"Not me," Angie countered in a small voice. Shamefacedly she remembered her cocky self-confidence . . . could it really have been only yesterday?

Joseph found himself moving across the galley. His oilskin trailed water across the linoleum, and when he stopped in front of Angie and slipped his arms around her, puddles formed at their feet. He held her as closely as he was able, allowing for the bulky life jackets.

"A good storm makes believers out of the best of us," he said gently. "You can't really call yourself a fisherman until you've been through a few."

Angie was still for a moment, snug in the cocoon of strength and security that his arms created. Then she shuddered, burying her face in the plump cushion of his life jacket. "You know, it was the strangest thing, but I saw something out there on deck. I saw—" She stopped.

Joseph smoothed the damp, frizzed hair away from her face. "Tell me what you saw," he suggested.

And so she did. "It was terrible," she concluded after the whole bizarre tale had tumbled out. "I saw it all, but there was nothing I could do. The men..."

There was agony in her voice, remembering the horror of the scene. "They were so afraid, I could tell, but so brave, too. They never gave up hope, even though there was no hope left, and they had to have known it...."

Her voice fell lower. "The windows were smashed in the wheelhouse, and seawater was washing over Cappy, and he just stood there, fighting that wheel like there was still something he could do. Then he...he shouted something, and then he was...gone. I felt the water rushing into my nose and my mouth—it felt as though *I* was the one who was drowning. And then...I saw Mano...."

"Yes?"

Angie's voice fell so low that Joseph had to bend his head to hear. "He was in the water. He was thrashing around, trying to stay afloat. He fought so hard, but the seas were so enormous—they kept driving him under. He came up struggling for air, but it took longer each time. He looked so tired! And then just for an instant I...I saw a flash of gold on his hand. It was his wedding band—"

She looked at Joseph wide-eyed, as if asking him to explain it. "And then he just kind of... let go, and he just... slipped away." She was crying now, not the great, wrenching, desperate sobs of grief, but the quiet, profound tears of acceptance. Joseph continued to pet her hair.

"It was so terrible," Angie whispered in a quavering voice. "At first. But at the last it was only..."

"Only what?"

"Peaceful."

She sounded peaceful, too, and for that Joseph was grateful. He brushed a gentle thumb under her eyes, where a few teardrops still clung precariously to the lower lashes. "What do you think it was that your father shouted, there at the end?" he asked.

Angie sniffed, then inelegantly swiped at her nose with the back of one hand. She looked at Joseph with a poignant twist of her lips. "What do men say at a time like that?" she said. "It could have been *'Charlotte,'* I guess. Maybe *'I love you.'*" Her sad smile broadened tenderly. "But knowing Cappy, it was probably *'Damn.'*"

Joseph was not as astonished as he might have been. He discounted nothing—he'd heard stories stranger than the one Angie had just related from old salts far more seasoned than she. A good storm makes believers out of the best of us, he reminded himself again, even those hardy few who pride themselves on their skepticism.

He wondered if somehow, someway, Long Jack had known his daughter needed him, and had gathered himself together one last time, from wherever the four winds had scattered his soul and the ocean currents had scattered his bones, to help her put him to rest for good?

Of course Joseph couldn't explain it—not to himself, and certainly not to Angie, but his heart was relieved. Her ghosts were buried. He knew that whatever else resulted from her stint aboard his vessel, at least she'd accomplished that.

"That was a brave thing you did out there today," he said softly. "But I'd rather lose a million cranes overboard than endanger...one of my crew."

Angie didn't know whether it was the words of praise that began a thawing of the ice that had settled into her very bones, or the strong arms in their wet, rubber sleeves wrapped firmly around her shoulders. Neither did she care. All she cared about was that she felt safe for the first time since this dreadful day had begun. Safe.

Joseph moved his hands under her damp hair and let his palms lightly caress her face.

"You were beautiful," he whispered, softer still. His tone was suddenly as intimate as the fingers that had tangled themselves in her unkempt hair. "In that yellow oilskin and those ridiculous boots flapping around your ankles—you were the most beautiful woman I've ever seen."

He flexed his big forearms, pressing her against him without removing his hands from her hair. Their bulky life jackets butted together, and under his breath Joseph uttered a frustrated oath.

He reached for the ties just below Angie's chin and jerked impatiently on one end; the knot unraveled in his hand. Then he looked her full in the face, his narrow, gray eyes glittering in the pale white light, asking permission to go further.

No, demanding permission to go further.

"But the storm . . . !"

"It's over, love. Or as good as. We rode it out. We're home free."

Angie couldn't detect any difference in the howling of the wind, no lessening of the pounding seas but if Joseph said it was over, she knew it must be.

Keeping his eyes fixed on hers, he carefully gauged her reaction as he reached lower with one deliberate hand and undid the buckle at her waist.

"But," she began a second time, "can you . . . ? Should you . . . ?"

"Madruga has the bridge," he replied brusquely. "I can. And I will."

He reached backward and dead-bolted the hatch with one decisive twist of his fingers. Then, still reading uncertainty in her eyes, he guessed another reason for her hesitation. He laughed, a single, harsh sound that was the first crack in the fiction of control he was struggling to maintain. "I was caught unprepared once," he growled roughly, with the faintest trace of a chuckle. "I won't be again."

That was all it took. Angie abandoned herself to his hands, and she quickly learned that he was as fully an expert in handling a woman as in everything else he did.

He lost no time divesting himself of his life jacket, pulling it over his head and dropping it to the floor. The oilskin came next, and it fell unnoticed on top of the orange vest. At last he reached for Angie's jacket, his fingers trembling at the proximity of her breasts, and lifted it over her head as reverently as if he expected to find her naked underneath.

When he brought his lips down on hers, Angie met them halfway, sampling his passion. Then she felt the hard edges of his teeth against her lips and she opened her mouth to let him enter. The heels of her palms tightened on the countertop as she rose to her toes, fitting the arched bow of her body to the hunkering curve of his.

There was something different about him tonight. He should have been exhausted. The white light of the emergency generator gave his skin an unnatural pallor. It shadowed his unshaven cheeks, making them look gaunt, but in spite of that he seemed exhilarated.

It occurred to Angie that he was like the weather. That balmy night in Puntarenas, he had been fair-weather—mellow, warm, humorous. On this tempestuous night he was tempestuous, too, and importunate and determined. She could tell by the insistence of his mouth on hers that, unlike the last time, he wouldn't wait *this* night.

The boat lurched and they staggered sideways. Joseph laughed again, a triumphant rumble from low in his throat, and it made Angie tremble with anticipation.

He loved the danger. He thrived on it. And as he adroitly backed her the few feet to her cabin door, his mouth still hard on hers, she knew that fair weather or foul, they were sailing directly into it.

Chapter Eighteen

The cabin was dark. Joseph, with his unerring knowledge of every inch of his boat, located the light fixture
in the ceiling. One hand released Angie just long
enough to pull the chain on the single bare bulb; then
he returned his big palm to the back of her head. He
held it immobilized while his fierce tongue probed the
hot wetness of her mouth.

His legs pushed purposefully against hers, guiding
her backward. Another step and Angie felt her bunk at
the back of her knees. Although the position was similar to dancing, it was nothing like the graceful two-step
they had shared in MamaLina's. Then he had held her
easily, allowing her to find her own rhythm; now he
held her hard against him, forcing her to adopt his
own.

One more step backward and Joseph, with an agile
twist of his torso, turned them around so that the bed
was behind him instead. He sat down on the edge and
drew Angie into the wide angle between his legs.

His eyes were on a level with her breasts. Remembering how they had looked that night in his quarters,
remembering how they had felt on the veranda at
MamaLina's, he ached to fit his mouth around the full,

brown tip of each one. Resolutely he forced himself to look upward and concentrate on her face. "There's something you have to know..." he began awkwardly.

The suggestion of a smile quirked her lips. "Are you sure you want to talk about it right now?" she teased throatily.

"No, I don't," he replied honestly. "But I think I'd better."

"Well, tell me, then, if it's so important." But she wrapped her arms around his head and buried his face against her stomach and pressed her cheek against his damp, curling hair, and suddenly there was nothing in the world that needed to be said.

Joseph groaned, knowing he'd just lost another battle with himself. He wondered derisively what had happened to his much-vaunted honor?

He fitted his hands around Angie's buttocks, pulling her even closer, and lifted his head to pursue with his lips the full, firm breasts that hung like fruit from a tree above his face. Ripe for the picking, his for the taking. Catching one nipple gently between his teeth he found, even through several layers of cloth, that it was already swollen and throbbing.

His hands moved from her bottom and began roving up and down her back, kneading it with ever-increasing urgency; then he slid them around to the front, where he tugged the tail of her chambray work shirt out of her jeans. Beneath the shirt, her skin was warm, and damp with rain, or saltwater or perspiration. Her body had the faint, powdery scent of talcum, intermingled with the tart aroma of seawater. Joseph had never smelled that unique combination on a woman before.

He clasped her waist with both his hands. His firm fingers made indentations in her soft skin and held her still while he breathed in the intoxicating smell. Then he began to reach upward under the fabric of her shirt, where he filled his hands with the cornucopia of her breasts.

His thumbs brushed lightly across the tips, still covered by the bra she had worn ever since the day on the speedboat deck when he had advised her on matters of dress. Each brush made Angie moan with helpless need. The soft cries filled his ears, driving out even the dreary tattoo of the rain.

The first contact of his fingers with her naked flesh had made Angie tremble. She wanted more. She wanted to feel his hot, urgent hands everywhere. Lifting her cheek from his hair, she put her hands on his shoulders and gently but firmly pushed him away.

"Wait just a minute," she whispered. She moved backward two short steps until she stood directly beneath the light, and with an unstudied instinct as old as humanity itself, began slowly and seductively to unbutton her shirt.

When that was done, she shrugged it off her shoulders, letting it drape from her elbows like a shawl. Then she unhooked the front closure of the bra. Freed, her magnificent breasts spilled out. The single bulb shining down gave them the honeyed sheen of ancient ivory. With a shy, proud smile, she lifted them in her hands and offered them to him.

It seemed to Joseph that he was moving in slow motion. Even the almost unendurable hardness in his groin throbbed slowly and ponderously. The single step from the bed to where Angie stood beneath the bare bulb was an interminable journey. Finally his fingers reached out and touched the longed-for flesh—flesh paler than the tanned skin that surrounded it, and smooth, and damp and warm.

Still in slow motion, he cupped his palms around the outthrust breasts and the loving, giving hands that offered them. As if in a dream, he lowered his head and kissed the ivory tops, then lifted them himself to kiss the softer, whiter, slightly damper flesh of the underside.

Angie held her breath. His seeking lips moved toward her taut, tumescent nipples; when he sucked one greedily into his mouth, she threw back her head and exhaled in a long, shuddering moan.

It inflamed Joseph. No more slow motion, no more reverence.

Quickly he thrust his hands into Angie's jeans, forcing the zipper open as he dragged them down her legs and threw them aside. Holding her as tightly as if she were a prize he'd just captured, he directed her forcefully to the bed and laid her down. Then he tore open his own jeans with the same controlled violence he'd used on hers. It was the violence that excited her; it was the control that made her trust him.

He stood over her for a moment, clad only in his rumpled blue shirt and damp T-shirt. His muscled thighs, almost on a level with Angie's eyes, looked even more powerful freed from the confining denim. The mat of hair that covered them was thick and dark, with a thicker, darker thatch curled at the juncture of his widespread legs. She saw the great, jutting thrust of him, and her throat worked convulsively. A need fully as basic and raw as his for her engulfed her. She wanted him inside her. That was all; it was the only thing.

She reached for his shirt with some vague notion about removing it, wanting him as naked as she was, but it was obvious that Joseph was long past caring about such refinements. He seized her wrist and held it while he bent over to retrieve a small foil packet from the pocket of his discarded jeans; then he knelt between her legs.

The white light behind him shadowed his skin, darkening the stubble on the flat planes of his jaw, transforming his craggy features into the dark, unrecognizable face of a stranger. But Angie wasn't looking at his face. Instead she watched as he opened the packet and rolled the silky circlet it contained over the shaft of his fierce, pendulous masculinity.

It was a continuation of the interrupted lovemaking at Puntarenas, starting right where that night had left off—past the words, past the first, tentative explorations of each other's bodies, past the gentleness. Now it was passion at its most basic, for him and for her. There was only the wanting and the needing, the sound of heavy breathing and the sudden, precipitous climb into ecstasy.

He rocked forward, supporting his weight on his straight arms, and flexed his buttocks and entered her. She felt the first thrust all the way up. "Oh, yes!" she moaned. She wrapped her legs around the pounding solidity of his body, tilting her hips upward to receive him. "Yes!"

The bedsprings sagged under their combined weight, and grated protestingly. Through the thin mattress Angie felt them like a metal grid against her back as Joseph drove her deeper and deeper into them. The squeaking of the bedsprings became louder and faster, a rhythmic accompaniment to the primitive choreography of their age-old and ageless mating dance.

Angie clasped her hands behind his neck and pulled his face down to meet her lips. She realized, as he stretched her and filled her and then with a harsh, guttural cry discharged his passion in a series of explosive contractions, how very, very long she'd been empty.

"HOW DO YOU *SLEEP* in this thing?" Joseph asked. His feet extended over the foot of Angie's short bunk, and he bumped them every time he tried to move.

"It's tricky," Angie admitted, "but I didn't expect luxuries."

"If you were a regular on one of my boats, I'd give you luxury." He kissed her playfully between words. One hand was splayed flat across her stomach, and one knee bent to lay possessively between her legs. "I'd have thick carpets on the floor—"

"Thick enough to make love on?"

"Of course. When we wanted to. And when we wanted to be more traditional, I'd have a big, round bed with a fur bedspread and lots of pillows. And I'd have mirrors all around, even on the ceiling, so that everywhere I looked I'd see you."

"And what would *I* do in quarters like that?"

"Not cook, that's for sure. You'd just wait—stay in bed all day long and wait for me. And I'd come in every chance I got and make love to you until you begged me to stop. And maybe I'd stop, and maybe I wouldn't...."

"You wouldn't stay a skipper long that way! The first time you came home with empty holds, Montero's would give you your walking papers!"

He traced one finger idly along the curve of her hip. "Would you mind that very much?"

"If you left Montero's? No, I wouldn't mind at all. You know Montero isn't one of my favorite people—"

"You don't know Montero."

"No, but I know enough about him. And I know there are certainly enough other fisheries that'd be willing to take on a skipper like you."

She felt his finger stop its dilatory skimming. "Well, it wouldn't be quite that simple," he said, with a laugh that sounded forced. "I guess I'll just have to let the mirrors wait for a few years."

Angie was sorry for the intrusion of business into the conversation. Obviously it made him uneasy. Loyalty, she thought—also not a bad trait in a skipper. No matter, her thoughts continued, there was plenty of time. She slipped her arm under Joseph's neck and cuddled his head in the deep valley of her cleavage. "That's okay, too," she said.

Gentle now, he lifted her breasts, one at a time, and closed his lips around the sweet, musky tips.

"Where does Madruga think you are?"

Joseph chuckled. "Sleeping. I said I'd relieve him at 0700 hours."

Over his shoulder, Angie glanced at her watch. "It's only five o'clock," she said. "Why don't you get some sleep? I'll wake you in time."

"Oh, lady," he protested. "I couldn't sleep now." But even while he spoke, his head grew heavy on her arm, then nodded a few times and came to rest in the hollow of her shoulder. Soft and warm and regular, his breath feathered lightly across her skin. Rain drummed monotonously on the hull of the *Sea Witch,* but inside the tiny former storeroom, the sound was muffled and far away.

Not wanting to disturb Joseph by getting up to turn off the light, not wanting to move at all, Angie nestled him closer and shaded his sleeping eyes with her hand.

Chapter Nineteen

"I seen worse," boasted Dominic to no one in particular. He, Pinheiro and Tennessee were swabbing the main deck in the aftermath of the typhoon. "Once I spent three days in the drink. Off Peru, it was. Russian trawler picked me up. Didnt know what they was doin' there. Didnt care."

"You never did, old man!" Pinheiro scoffed. "You got so much blubber on you, you'd a'spent three days in the water, sharks would'a had a feast!"

"Ask Angie! It was with ol' Jack Reno!" He appealed to Angie, occupied in the passageway by the galley, wielding a mop of her own. "Tell 'em, girl! Yer granddaddy must'a told ye about it! Man dont fergit a thing like that!"

Angie straightened up, rested her hands on the handle of her mop and slouched on one hip. "Nope," she responded with a teasing grin. "He never told me."

It wasn't the worst storm any of them had weathered, but it had been bad enough. There was no damage to the *Sea Witch* herself, but several of the speedboats had been smashed by the rampaging crane and couldn't be repaired at sea. Joseph had no choice but to set a course for San Diego.

The trip home was like a vacation cruise. Sunny and idle and long.

Home. Angie knew that the word meant something different to everyone. To Pinheiro, it meant a newborn daughter, whose birth was announced via ship-to-shore radio five weeks out. To slow-talking Tennessee, it meant a wedding—his own. To Dominic, it meant one more trip he'd survived, one trip closer to his pension.

To Angie, it meant new beginnings. One was Joseph. Another was Reno's. Somehow in her mind, the two had become inextricably linked, and she was full of plans for both.

In the galley, during mealtimes or during one of the eternal poker games, Joseph treated her with the same careless detachment he always had. If an electric current passed between them when their fingers accidentally touched as she passed him a serving bowl or refilled his bottomless coffee cup, it was a magical moment kept between the two of them.

When she came onto the bridge, their conversations were brief and superficial, ever mindful of the listening ears of Madruga and Otis.

The nights were another story—secret hours of privacy in Angie's cabin, snatched between watches, but all the more exciting because of that.

Joseph was an imaginative and uninhibited lover, sometimes boyishly eager, at other times possessed of a dark, seemingly insatiable sensuality. To Angie's surprise, she found the same eagerness and the same sensuality in herself. It was a side of herself that she had never suspected, a side that Mano, in his own youth and inexperience, had had neither the knowledge nor the expertise to plumb.

But Joseph had both. He explored her body and her mind and her soul in such depth that she felt as though she had no secrets from him. And she knew that the way he gave himself to her, so completely and with no holding back, meant that he felt the same.

Only one thing disturbed Angie. Joseph didn't seem to think in terms of the future. He never spoke about next year, or next month or even next week when the *Sea Witch* would arrive back in San Diego. He appeared content to live in the here and now, taking their relationship, as he took life in general, one day at a time.

One night she asked him about it. It was an hour before dawn, when Joseph would relieve Madruga on the bridge and Angie would begin another day in the galley.

Joseph was naked and completely at ease that way, lying on a pillow propped against the bulkhead behind Angie's bunk. His long legs stretched the full length of the bunk, feet extended over the metal foot rail and crossed at the ankles. Angie was naked, too, curled in the crook of his arms.

Joseph was evasive. "It's the life we lead, you know that," he told her in reply. "What does the future hold but more goodbyes? I prefer to deal with the real world when I get back to it, and enjoy what we have right now."

Tennessee is planning for the future, she wanted to say. So is Pinheiro. But she didn't. Tennessee and Pinheiro were very young; neither did they have the first-hand experience of a marriage that had gone sour because of the demands of life in the fleet.

There were drawbacks to loving a fisherman, Angie reflected, and this was one of them. Life was lived two or three or four weeks at a time, then he was gone again. Angie understood it because it was the way she had been brought up, but that didn't mean she liked it. Especially not now, when she was so preoccupied with plans for herself and Joseph and Reno's, and wanted so much to share them.

She sighed resignedly. "I know. I know you'll only be in port a month, and then you'll be going east for the winter. I understand that...."

Joseph was silent for a moment. "Maybe I just won't go," he said finally.

"You mean let someone *else* take the *Sea Witch* east for the season?" She gave a skeptical laugh. "I don't think so. You're just like that old sailorman you told me about—you'll never break the chains that bind you to the sea."

Joseph looked surprised. "You understand that?"

She nodded. "Of course. I don't like it, but I understand it. I would never begrudge you that." *As long as I am the one you come home to.*

The idea, startling though it should have been, somehow seemed as natural as breathing. She sighed again. "Dominic told me I should get out of the fleet."

Joseph's arm tightened beneath her neck. "Sell Reno's, you mean?"

"Sell Reno's?" Angie twisted her head to look up at him and laughed gaily. "Whatever gave you that idea? No, he meant *marry* out of the fleet. A doctor, he said, or a lawyer."

"He may be right, you know." Joseph's voice was flat. "It's not much of a life for a woman."

Angie thought briefly of the woman who had been his wife, the woman who hadn't been able to take it.

"Maybe not," she said fiercely, in answer to that other woman as well as to Joseph. "But it's *my* life! I wouldn't want any other. Don't you see? It's the kind of life you lead that's made you what you are. And I wouldn't have you any other way." Privately she suspected the reason she had fallen in love with Joseph so quickly and so completely was that she had loved the *kind* of man he was even before she knew he *was* that kind of man.

She rolled over onto her stomach and propped herself on her elbows, resting her chin on his chest. "It was the same with Cappy," she added thoughtfully. "I guess what I loved about him was, in a way, what killed him."

"You wouldn't wonder about that with me?"

Angie clapped her hand over his mouth. "Don't say that!" Her response was instinctive. "It's bad luck!"

When she realized how much she sounded like her old *avo,* she laughed ruefully. "You think you've left the old ways behind, and then, the minute you let your guard down, you find that you've carried them right along with you!"

"I wouldn't worry about it," Joseph replied, lowering his chin to kiss her forehead. "It's just another way of saying 'think positive.' I'm sure you're not in any danger of regressing back to the Middle Ages." He slid down on the pillow and rolled Angie on top of him, spreading her thighs with his knees.

"Do we have time?" she asked practically, glancing at her watch, but already she felt the magic beginning. She gripped his shoulders, pushing herself upright so that she straddled his hips. Her back was curved, suspending her breasts within easy reach of his mouth, and her head was bent so that her tousled hair fell forward, hiding her face.

Joseph reached up with infinite care to tuck the flyaway curls behind her ears. With the same care, his hands slid down her body to cup her buttocks, to lift her and then lower her onto his turgid rigidity. After that he did nothing but lie still and stay hard for her, letting her make love to him, letting her set the pace. Impaled, unable to move except for the tight, circular motion of her pelvis against his, Angie breathed a visceral sigh of satisfaction and abandoned herself to sensation.

She loved everything about him, although she hadn't used that word yet. At least not to him. She loved his raw good looks. She loved his demeanor, so reserved in public, so expressive when they were alone.

She loved his bronzed torso, the way his muscles opposed each other when he moved to give him an angular grace. And she loved the tight bunches in his diaphragm and stomach, the way they rippled against her skin when she lay stretched out on top of him. She loved his heavy maleness.

And afterward, when the maleness was soft and relaxed and vulnerable, pliant enough to lie still in her hand, she loved that, too.

ANGIE WAS READING in her usual spot on the speedboat deck when Dominic's grizzled gray head bobbed over the edge.

His giant tortoise shell was propped on his back; and with his dark, seamed face poking out from the top of the shell, his gnarled hands and horny feet protruding from the sides, he looked very much like the shell's original inhabitant as he crawled slowly up the ladder.

"Use some comp'ny, Angie girl?"

"Sure." She slid over. "Still working on your shell?"

"Takes time," he grunted. "Like ever'thin' else worthwhile." He bent his head to his task, attacking the shell with his old chamois cloth and a generous amount of elbow grease. Angie returned to her book.

After a few silent moments, Dominic cleared his throat.

Angie glanced up inquiringly, but found his attention concentrated on the shell in his lap. After another few minutes, he cleared his throat again.

"Something on your mind, Dominic?"

Dominic cleared his throat a third time. "Ye know how I feel about ye," he began hesitatingly. "Like my *filha,* my own daughter. Ye know that?"

"Yes, I know that."

He continued to polish energetically, keeping his eyes fixed on the shell. "This skipper, like I told ye, he's a good man, and he can find fish. But...I would hate to see ye hurt, and me the only one what can talk to ye. I wouldn't feel square with yer daddy when I meet him again someday, may it be many years from now." Fervently he rapped his knuckles on the wooden deck.

"What are you trying to tell me, Dominic?"

"Ye maybe think yer in love with this skipper. An' maybe ye think he loves ye, too...."

Angie's cheeks flamed. They had tried so hard to be discreet! "Is that what the men are saying?"

"No!" Dominic exploded indignantly. "No one says it! Only *I* say it. Because I see ye, I watch ye. Because ye are *filha* to me. And because Long Jack was my friend."

There was no hurrying Dominic, Angie thought, but in this instance that was probably a blessing—it gave her time to think up a response.

"He is a good man, like I say. But Long Jack he is not. Mano he is not. He is from San Pedro!"

As if all the evils of the world came from San Pedro! "A lot of people come from San Pedro" was all Angie said aloud. "I don't think that's reason enough to—"

"There are *other* reasons!" Dominic sputtered. "There are *other* reasons," he repeated in a more placating tone. "We will be home soon. Talk to yer mama, let her tell ye."

"Tell me what? That men from San Pedro are not to be trusted?" She smiled. "Don't worry about me, Dominic. I'm a grown woman now. My mother would be the first to say so."

"Grown, *sim*. But not until ye are old like me will ye understand the blackness in men's hearts!"

Angie looked at the old man, trying not to let the irritation she felt show through. He wasn't really trying to interfere, she told herself. He was just doing his duty, and in the world as he knew it, he had not only the right, but the obligation.

"I appreciate your concern, Dominic. You've done your duty by my father *and* me. I'll certainly give some thought to what you say."

Dominic glowered, knowing that he and his advice were being courteously disregarded. That was the difficulty in growing old, he thought gloomily. The strength of age is wisdom, the Portuguese say. But the young no longer paid attention. He sighed. Suddenly he felt very old, indeed.

EVERY SAILING and every return, Cappy used to say after a few glasses of Madeira, meant more hellos and goodbyes. Goodbyes to men who were closer in a way than family, and hellos to families, more loved but never as close as the men who had, for a little while, held each other's lives in their hands.

The crew didn't gather so much in the galley after meals. They found places quieter and more isolated. In the evenings they would gather on the foredeck and watch the sun go down. Sometimes they told stories that grew more elaborate with each telling. Other times, Dominic would break out his harmonica and Pinheiro his guitar, and they would lead the men in the old songs—the rousing, ribald ones at first, but always ending with the traditional sea chanties, the plaintive expressions of an essentially lonely way of life.

Late into the night they would sit, leaning against the gunwale, each wrapped in his own, private thoughts, until one by one they would flick their cigarettes overboard and go silently, moodily, to bed.

Long after everyone else had left, Dominic would remain. And from her cabin, Angie would hear the thin wail of his harmonica, barely audible over the rumble of the diesels as it echoed across the dark water and was lost at sea.

Chapter Twenty

One bright, hot morning, the *Sea Witch* came home.

When the boat was tied up at Cannery Row, the crew began unloading the catch. They heaved the ice-cold tuna onto conveyer belts at the loading dock that would carry them from the holds into the cannery. Once the off-loading was underway, Joseph joined Angie on the main deck. Discreetly he slipped his arm around her waist and together they watched the enormous fish roll by.

It wasn't much to show for nearly three months of hard work, Angie couldn't help but think. For once she was glad that the crew had a big-time outfit like Montero Maritime behind them to soften the disappointment of a slow season.

"Do you pay the men now?" she asked Joseph.

"No," he replied. "Montero's mails them a check."

"I remember Cappy with his briefcase full of new one-hundred-dollar bills, counting them out by the thousands. It was so exciting!" *The old days.*

"That was a simpler time. Now computers keep track of everything. Besides, how many men do you suppose got home without dropping a fair amount in half a dozen bars along Lower Broadway? It's much more efficient like this."

"We still pay the old way at Reno's." There was a wistful note in her voice.

"Well, Reno's has a lot of tradition behind it," Joseph said, smiling down at her. "Are you happy to be home? You *look* happy."

"You don't," she replied. For the first time she noticed the morose expression on his face. "Is something bothering you?"

"Not really. It's just that now the paperwork starts, and that's never been my favorite part of the job."

"Will you be finished in time for dinner?"

"I'll make a point of it."

She leaned over and kissed him lightly on the cheek. He looked startled.

"Don't worry." She laughed. "We're legal now, remember? As far as anyone can tell, I'm just the girl you left behind, welcoming you home."

"If that's the case—" he put his arm around her and pulled her close "—please welcome me home properly. It's been three months...." He planted a breathtaking kiss on her lips, in full view of any bystanders who might be looking their way, and then released her.

"I love you, Reno," he said softly. It was the first time he'd spoken those words outside the intimacy of darkness and the throes of passion, and they sounded tentative and almost shy, as if he were not sure how they would come across in the clear light of day.

"I love you, too."

"Go now. I've got a lot to wade through if I'm going to be finished by tonight."

"I'll pick you up—what time? Say eightish?"

"Say sevenish. I don't think I can make it 'til eigh-tish."

"Sevenish it is, then." Leaning over, she kissed his cheek. "I can't wait," she whispered huskily. Then she hoisted her seabag, slung it over her shoulder and crossed the gangplank to Market Street.

Once on the other side, she looked back at Joseph, standing alone on the deck of the *Sea Witch.* Cappy had looked so different at the end of a trip, sur-rounded by his crew as he counted crisp, new one-hundred-dollar bills into their hands—laughing, jok-ing, slapping the men on the backs and signing them up for the next season. Joseph somehow just looked lonely.

He looked more than just lonely, she realized. He looked as though he'd lost his last friend.

It was Montero's, she decided. It had been a bad trip catchwise, and Montero's was probably going to be very unhappy with him. The camaraderie, the sup-port, the sharing of the bad times as well as the good— the very basis, in fact, of life in the fleet—was lacking in a big-time outfit like that.

Joseph would be much happier when he signed on with Reno's!

Impulsively she turned, jogging backward a few steps to blow him a kiss. "So long, sailor!" she called.

Joseph smiled and waved back. When she turned around and disappeared into the throng of passersby on Market Street, he sobered again. How would she feel when she knew who he really was? Not like blow-ing kisses to him over the heads of strangers, of that much he was certain.

If only he hadn't made love to her, he told himself, furious at his own weakness, he might have stood a chance. A slim one, maybe, but at least a chance. Now he knew exactly what she'd think, and what was worse, she'd have every right in the world to think it.

CHARLOTTE LOOKED UP when the office door opened. She pulled her glasses off her face and tossed them on the desk in front of her.

"Baby..." She rose and walked slowly around the desk. "I didn't know you were back." She reached out to touch a lock of Angie's hair. "Your pretty hair...it's all bleached out. And your face...so dark."

She held out her arms and without a word, Angie went into them.

CHARLOTTE WANTED to hear everything, and Angie was glad to oblige. As she had in the old days when Cappy came home, Charlotte laughed and cried and commiserated and scolded.

"I know I did a good job," Angie concluded. "And I could tell the men respected that. Whether it's going to do Reno's any good or not remains to be seen. I also got a lot of firsthand lessons in how to work with the men, and I think that'll come in handy in the future."

"And what about this...Joseph?" Charlotte asked with an discerning smile. "You're in love with him?"

Angie colored. "Why do you say that?" she demanded.

Charlotte laughed. "My dear, you never stopped talking about him!"

"But I haven't said anything about love."

"Baby, everything you said, said it!"

"There's something," Angie admitted. "It's just that we haven't *talked* about it yet. But now that we're home—"

"*You're* home, baby. He's not. His home is in San Pedro, remember? Three months—it's a very short acquaintance to begin talking about love."

"You *married* Cappy on a shorter one," Angie reminded her mother.

Charlotte laughed; then her face became thoughtful. "Of course, the other thing is...the problem is..."

"I know. He works for Montero."

Charlotte pursed her lips speculatively. "If he's everything you seem to think he is, I wonder how he would feel about throwing his lot in with Reno's?" Retrieving the yellow pencil she kept tucked behind her ear, she tapped her pursed lips with the eraser end. "It could work," she said. "With our own skipper in our pocket, we might be able to overcome some of the chauvinism we keep running into." She raised her eyebrows at Angie. "What do you think?"

Angie remembered Joseph's aversion to discussing the future. "He's very...*loyal* to Montero's," she said.

"Well, it's something we can keep in mind for the future." Charlotte wisely let the subject drop. "Bring him home, baby. I'd like to see what this Joseph is made of."

"MY MOTHER WANTS to meet you," Angie said to Joseph, reporting the conversation later. "She asked me to bring you home for dinner some night."

They were seated in the dining room of The Cloisters, a small, out-of-the-way inn that was Joseph's choice whenever he stayed in San Diego. The food was excellent and the wine from their own vineyards.

"I like it here because I'm fascinated by wine making," he had told Angie on the drive out of the city to

The Cloisters' rural setting. "I do a little of it myself, in a very small way."

"Odd hobby for a fisherman," Angie said, smiling. "When do you find the time?"

He laughed, the gentle, ironic laugh that so frequently seemed to be directed at himself. "Well, maybe I enjoy it because it forces me to *take* the time. Patience isn't one of my virtues, but there's just no way you can rush the grapes!"

The inn had once been a monastery, and it still had the hushed, other-worldly quality of a church. High, latticed windows ringed the dining room, which had been the refectory, and candles cast evocative shadows on the thick, adobe walls.

Joseph had told Angie a little about the history of the place. "The brothers," he'd said, "earned their daily bread by making wine for all the Catholic diocese from Escondido to the Mexican border. Then times changed—" he smiled wryly "—as times have a tendency to do.

"The bishops found that they could import wine from New York cheaper than they could buy it from the good brothers, and wine production at The Cloisters went into a slump. So the brothers decided to supplement their income by providing a roadside retreat for weary travelers, with their excellent wine as both an inducement and a sideline."

Now, of course, the inn was run by a national hotel chain and the vineyards overseen by professionals, but they hadn't yet managed to destroy the medieval ambience that made The Cloisters so unique.

Angie had dressed for dinner. She wore a swath of white silk that skimmed her body and fell below her knees, simple as a nun's habit except for the low-cut princess neckline. Her upswept hair was secured by a golden clip, and cascaded from the crown of her head to the nape of her neck in a mass of ebony curls.

Joseph had dressed, too, in the white linen jacket that he had worn in Puntarenas, now neatly pressed, and pleated navy slacks. The clothes didn't emphasize his powerful physique the way his tunaman's uniform did, but he wore them with a natural elegance that belied his occupation.

When the maître d' showed them to their table, he had shuffled on silent, slippered feet. The waiter who brought their drinks and their dinner had also shuffled; so silent were his movements that he might have been a monk himself.

Now, over an elegant Salmon Wellington with parsley cream sauce and wild artichoke rice, Joseph seemed provoked by the turn the conversation had taken.

"My mother wants to meet you," Angie repeated, thinking his silence meant that he hadn't heard. "She asked me to invite you home for dinner—"

"Do we have to talk about your mother just now?" he interrupted tersely.

"Of course not. We can talk about anything you like." But her voice was bewildered.

He took her hand and lifted it to his lips over the dry, fruity St. Benedictius Chenin Blanc. "I love you, Angie. You love me. Does it matter so much what your mother thinks?"

"Of course not, only..." There it was again, the future they had never talked about. "I mean, if for some reason she *didn't* like you, it wouldn't change the way I feel. But she *will.*" Angie smiled earnestly. "She already *does!* All she needs to do is put a face to the name...."

Yes, that's all *she needs to do!* Joseph was angered by the panic he felt overtaking his normally unflappable mind.

He had fully intended to make a clean breast of everything, to confess the whole incredible farce to Angie over dinner. This ancient monastery, he thought with black humor, lent itself very well to that sort of thing!

He hoped she'd see the humor in the situation. He hoped she'd laugh. Barring that, at least in this public place she probably wouldn't throw the breadsticks at him before he'd had a chance to explain. But now the waiter had shuffled up with the dessert menu in hand, and still Joseph hadn't found the necessary words.

"Dessert?" the waiter murmured softly.

"I think not," Joseph said. "Just our check, please." Under his breath he added, "I have other plans for dessert."

To Angie, his implication was crystal clear, and she was every bit as disconcerted as if the silent, shuffling waiter were really a monk.

THE VALET BROUGHT Angie's little sports car around to the fortresslike entryway of the inn and automatically gave the keys to Joseph, who then dropped them into Angie's hand.

"Where to?" Angie asked.

Joseph considered the question. "Well, I'd like to get naked with you as soon as possible," he said, experiencing an abrupt escalation of the anticipation he had been trying to curb all evening. "I don't suppose you'd consider a sleazy motel . . . ?"

"Only as a last resort," Angie bantered in return. "We have no luggage. . . ."

"Okay, then, how about a fancy hotel downtown?"

"Same problem. No luggage. You know how desk clerks frown on that sort of thing...."

Joseph lifted his shoulders in a fatalistic shrug. "Well, I guess that leaves us no other choice, then."

"The *Sea Witch?*"

"Afraid so."

"I was hoping you'd say that!" Angie turned the key in the ignition, put the car in gear and headed in the direction of the waterfront.

"DRINK?" JOSEPH ASKED, after Angie parked her car on the dock and they had walked to the snug harbor of Joseph's stateroom.

"Do you have any of that Montero brandy left?"

"Coming right up," he replied, going into the kitchen. When he returned, he carried a snifter half-full of Montero's finest in each hand. He presented one of the goblets to Angie, where she stood with one elbow resting gracefully on the breakfast bar.

Joseph watched the muscles of her throat work as she swallowed the brandy. Her neck was slender, he observed appreciatively. It formed a long column of tanned flesh from the tip of her upraised chin to the top of her daring décolletage. At the hollow of her throat throbbed a tender blue vein that virtually begged for the attention of his mouth.

The white silk was a stark contrast to her olive skin, the rich curves of breasts and hips a stark contrast to the slender column of her neck. In her high-heeled pumps and upswept hair, her head nearly grazed the ceiling. An Amazon, Joseph said to himself, and felt the thickness rising in him.

He took a sip of the brandy. "Your hair pinned up like that ... I like it. Of course, I liked it down, too, frizzing out like you'd stuck your finger in an electrical socket—"

"It never looked that bad! Did it?"

"And I love the perfume, although the sweat was every bit as sexy."

"I didn't sweat!"

"You did. But beneath that dress is the same body, isn't it? The same one that hid out under the jeans and wrinkled shirts and tried to pretend it was a man's?" He held up his glass. "To us," he pronounced. "And to life in the real world."

With a suggestive half smile, he dipped the tip of his forefinger into the brandy and rubbed it against Angie's lips; she sucked the tart sweetness from his finger. He dipped his finger again and placed a golden drop behind each of her ears, then lazily licked both drops away.

Finally he put a single drop between her breasts, where the low-cut princess neckline offered a shadowed glimpse of what it concealed. Bending his head, he proceeded to lick that away, too. Angie held her breath as he pursued it with slow, leisurely flicks of his tongue.

Then, both hands wrapped around the bowl of his goblet, Joseph turned and walked to the other side of the stateroom. He sat down on the couch, leaned backward into the cool leather cushions and crossed his legs at the knees. He regarded Angie from beneath heavy, half-closed lids.

"That dress is beautiful on you," he said. "You should always wear white." He paused. "Please take it off."

Without a word, Angie placed her glass on the bar. Then slowly, seductively, exquisitely aware of every movement of her body, she reached behind and unzipped the long back zipper. One sinuous twist and the dress was a silken white pool at her feet. She smiled. Waited.

Joseph's heavy-lidded eyes watched her coolly. "Now the slip." His voice cracked on the last word, and her smile widened. The magic was beginning.

When the slip followed the dress, she stood before him clad only in panty hose and pumps.

"Come here," he then instructed, and she crossed the plush blue carpet to where he sat. Waiting. She glided rather than walked, emphasizing the womanly sway of her body as she unhurriedly placed one foot in front of the other.

When she finally stood before him, he reached up to caress her face. "I was so afraid I'd imagined you," he said huskily, "I was afraid I'd get back and you'd be gone. Like a mermaid...."

Running his hands down her body, he reassured himself of her size, her shape, her presence. "Like that goddess who demands payment in gold...." He fumbled in the pocket of his dinner jacket and produced a small, velvet box. Silently he placed it in Angie's hands.

Nestled on the blue satin in the box was what appeared to be a handful of tiny diamonds. But when Angie took them between her fingers she discovered that it was a necklace—many strands of faceted diamonds, irregularly strung on a gold cord so thin as to be nearly invisible.

"Oh, Joseph!" she gasped in awe. "It's lovely!" Lifting it out of the box, she held it suspended from one hand, where it spiraled slowly in the air, catching the light and reflecting it in a thousand tiny prisms. "I've never seen anything so lovely!" She looked at him wide-eyed, etiquette forgotten. "But you can't afford..."

"It's my price of admission," he said solemnly.

"But—!"

He ignored her astonished protests. "Here, let me hook it for you." He turned her around so that she faced the mirror over the couch, then took the fragile thing in his hands and stepped behind her to fasten the clasp. The diamonds around her neck looked like droplets of water shimmering on her skin.

"It reminded me of you," he said, as their eyes met in the mirror. "Rising out of the water like a gift from the sea." Their eyes still joined in the mirror, Joseph bent his head forward and kissed her bare shoulder.

Angie slipped off the pumps and the panty hose, but kept the necklace on as she sat on the edge of the couch. The leather was cold against her thighs.

She reached for him and he felt her fingers unzip the front of his trousers. Coward! he berated himself harshly, as his own fingers tangled convulsively in her hair. His last coherent thought—before she took him in her mouth, before his breath came in a series of long, shuddering groans, before waves of sensation rocked him to his toes and rendered him unable to think at all—was that once again he wasn't going to be able to tell her.

Chapter Twenty-One

The situation at Reno's was even worse than Angie had feared.

"The way I see it," Angie, slouched dispiritedly behind one desk in the cluttered office, announced to her mother, who sat ramrod straight behind the other. "We can either make the interest payments or eat."

"It's been that way for some time now," Charlotte confessed. "I've been able to get extensions from the bank, but the last time they were quite reluctant. I don't think they're going to carry us much longer."

Mother and daughter looked at each other somberly. The dusty venetian blind was raised at a crooked angle to admit the sights and sounds of the bustling wharf outside. Business as usual for some, Angie thought grimly, but not for us. Not for us. The ancient watercooler in the corner burbled in mournful agreement.

"Well," she continued aloud, "the only solution I see is to sell one of the boats. It'll cut down on our profit, but if we can reduce overhead more than that, it might get us through the winter."

"I've had the same thought. It's like cutting away a piece of my life, but if it'll buy us a little time..."

Charlotte drummed her fingers thoughtfully on her desk. "There isn't time to put it up for bids. We might offer it to WesPac. They'd rather buy us outright, but they'd probably settle for a piece at a time."

There was a suspicious catch in her voice. Digging out a handkerchief from the sleeve of her cardigan, she blew her nose noisily.

"It's only a temporary setback." Angie willed confidence into her words. "If we have as good a winter run as we did the summer, we should be all right."

"Of course we will," Charlotte echoed with the same false bravado.

THAT EVENING in his quarters aboard the *Sea Witch*, Joseph was less optimistic. "It might work," he conceded, "if you can get a good price for the boat. Which one are you thinking of selling?"

"The *Skipjack*."

"Too old. Sell one of the newer ones—the *Dago Red,* maybe. There's more life in her, and you'll be able to get a better price. Keep the *Skipjack*. If the season's any good at all, she'll bring in almost as much as the *Dago Red,* and that's what you need most right now."

"The *Dago Red* was the last boat Cappy had built. It was his pride and joy." And he had mortgaged Reno's to the hilt to pay for it. They were still paying for it; that was one of the major sources of their financial difficulties.

"This is no time for sentiment, love. You can build another *Dago Red* someday. Your back's to the wall here."

"You're right, of course."

"And don't offer her to WesPac. Put her up for bid."

"But it has to be done before the winter season begins!"

"Offer her to Montero's, then. They'll do better by you than WesPac."

"Montero's?" Angie's voice rose an octave. "What in the world makes you think that?"

"Come on, Angie," he said, a trace of something that sounded like anger in his tone. "Whatever else you may think about Montero, have you ever heard that he's dishonest?"

"No-o-o," she replied slowly. "I guess not. It's just that I don't like dealing with people like that. They're like machines. No heart and no soul." She sighed. "I hate what they've done to our industry, that's all."

"It's just business, love. You've faced worse things in your life than a few stodgy old men in business suits." Looking at her more closely, he noticed tired smudges under her eyes. He put his arm around her shoulder. "Rough day?" he asked.

"No, not really." She sighed again. "It's just that we lost Amador today."

"I'm sorry to hear that."

"So was I. He's going to work for Montero. It seems that *everyone* is going to work for Montero, these days." Her voice was bitter. "Every time we get a good man we lose him, to Montero or to some other outfit up along the coast."

"What did Amador make last year on the *Charlotte E.?*"

Angie glanced away. "I know, I know. You can't blame a man for trying to better himself." But she knew that she did blame him, and everyone else who had left Reno's like rats deserting a sinking ship.

"I know you think conglomerates are the wave of the future," she challenged Joseph in an eruption of frustration. "But it doesn't *have* to be that way! Our ancestors didn't come here to pour their life's blood into some anonymous corporation! They did it for themselves, and for their children. Us! To work twenty-four hours a day, the way my father did, and his father and *his* father, it's... it's..." Her voice lost some of its steam. "Well, you wouldn't know about that."

She knew she was being unfair. After all, just because Joseph believed that aquabusiness was the wave of the future didn't mean he was responsible for it!

Abruptly he stood and walked across the room. He propped his hands on either side of the porthole and fixed his gaze on the sailboats that skimmed the bay like great white birds. "You're wrong, you know. I *do* know about that, and I admire it. But times change. In a few years there won't be room for small fisheries like Reno's. I think we'll lose something very important when that happens. But I'm not going to hide my head in the sand and pretend it *isn't* happening."

Modern technology and competition from foreign markets was transforming the industry—there was no doubt about that. Soon it would bear little resemblance to the way of life Long Jack, or his father or *his* father knew. Still, it was inconceivable to Angie that anyone but a Reno would be running Reno Fisheries.

"But it isn't inevitable!" she cried passionately. "We can turn it around! And when others see us doing it, they'll join us—!"

"Not Reno's."

That brought her up short like a slap in the face. "Why *not* Reno's?"

"Because Reno's has lost its rudder. With Long Jack, you might have held on—for a while. But without him, you have no one at the helm who knows how to sail the ship. Tuna—it's more than a degree in business. It's an . . . intuition. Not many men have it. Long Jack did. But Reno's doesn't have it anymore, and everyone in the fleet knows it, except you."

A silence fell, lengthened uncomfortably.

"Do *you* have it?" Angie finally asked.

Joseph's voice was diffident. "I hope someday I will."

"Well, then, why don't you use it for your own benefit?" Angie jumped to her feet and joined him at the porthole. "Haven't you ever thought about owning your own boat?"

Despite her attempt to sound practical, her voice rushed on with an eagerness that was decidedly unbusinesslike. "With Amador gone, we're going to need another captain. Of course we couldn't offer you what you get from Montero's, but you'd be a partner! And later we can think about expanding. My father and my grandfather both left Reno's bigger than when they took over, and I mean to do the same. In a few years—"

Joseph held up a restraining hand. "Let me get this straight. You want me to buy into Reno's?"

"Well, yes," Angie said, and even to her own ears her voice sounded defensive. "You don't need to decide right away, of course. But it . . . it could work, don't you think?"

"What would your mother say to that?"

"She mentioned it first! Frankly, she knows that if you work for Montero's, you've got to be good. That's the only kind of man they hire." Angie was stung by what she perceived to be his singular lack of enthusiasm. Why did he look as though she were offering him a spot on the guillotine? *Why didn't he say something?*

Joseph clenched his hands against the cool brass frame that surrounded the porthole. The corded tendons on his wrist stood out like ropes. "My love, I can't!" he cried. Then he regained control. "I can't leave Montero's, Angie," he said more calmly. "It's just not that simple."

"That's odd," she retorted. "Aboard the *Sea Witch* you were willing—eager, even—to give up Montero's for me."

"Aboard the *Sea Witch,* a million miles from the real world, everything was possible. It's...different now."

He was different now from the man he had been at sea. He was no longer just fair-weather or foul; now he was full of eddys and shoals, uncharted depths and unknown currents. His reluctance to meet Charlotte, for example, had solidified into frank avoidance, and Angie could find no explanation for it. At first she thought he was simply afraid Charlotte might not approve of him, but even after Angie's repeated assurances, he found one transparent excuse after another to refuse Angie's frequent invitations to her home.

"You mean it's easier to love when there are no distractions?" she said caustically.

Joseph took her obstinate body in his arms. "I mean that I don't want to talk about your mother right now," he said. "And I don't want to talk about Reno's, either."

He knew he was being brutally dishonest. If she knew the truth, she'd spit in his eyes instead of offering him a partnership in her beloved fishery. Joseph, feeling himself sinking deeper and deeper into a trap of his own making, knew that time was running out.

He took Angie's stubborn chin between thumb and forefinger. "Look, you do whatever you feel you have to do about Reno's. I wish I could help you, but it's just not something I can do. I don't want to quarrel."

"I don't, either," she mumbled stubbornly. "But—"

"The reason I don't want to quarrel," he continued doggedly, "is because I have to go away tomorrow."

Her mood immediately changed. "Oh, Joseph, so soon?"

"I have to take the *Sea Witch* up to San Pedro so they can get a crew ready for the winter season. And I have to make my reports, file my paperwork—things like that. Then I'll come back to you. And we'll talk, okay?"

"When you come back, it'll be time to *leave* for the winter run," Angie pointed out sourly. "And then it'll be Christmas, and right after the first of the year you'll be leaving again...."

He kissed her lightly on one corner of her mouth, then on the other. "When I come back we'll find the time, I promise." His hands fell persuasively, fitting themselves around her buttocks with bold familiarity. His voice also fell persuasively. "Right now I want to love you."

"That won't solve anything," Angie protested, but of course it did, at least temporarily. Already she felt her traitorous body weakening, and almost immediately melted into the curve of his embrace.

Over her head, the expression on Joseph's face was bleak. When, he wondered, had he developed this talent for deceit? What did he expect would change between now and two weeks from now? He had no idea. He was buying a little time, that was all; he was hoping for a miracle, when all his experience had taught him nothing if not how unlikely were the chances of divine intercession.

Chapter Twenty-Two

There was a perfunctory knock at the door of Reno's office, and Georgie Correia bounced in. With his usual irritating aplomb, he plopped into one of the cracked vinyl armchairs and flashed Angie a wide, professional smile.

A smudge of carbon on her cheek and a pencil behind one ear, she glanced up at him suspiciously. She threw the pencil down on the desk in front of her, pushed her chair back from the desk and folded her hands in her lap with barely concealed impatience. "All right, Georgie," she said. "What do you want?"

"Is that any way to greet an old friend? I just came by to say 'hello.' Haven't seen you since you got back, not for lack of trying, I might add."

Angie eyed him skeptically.

"And, er, also to see how you're getting on with the business. I heard you sold the *Dago Red*."

"You heard correctly." Montero Maritime had purchased the *Dago Red*, as Joseph had said they would, and for a much higher price than Angie would have dared ask. The profit would get them through the winter.

"But why to Montero? I thought you *hated* Montero!" Behind the rimless glasses his eyes assumed an artless expression. "You should have given us a chance. WesPac would've done all right by you, you know that."

"You know, Georgie," Angie said, as if an idea had just occurred to her. "You annoy me on several different levels. One is the way you sneak up on a subject. What's really on your mind?"

"Reno's. Lunch. You. Not necessarily in that order."

"Sorry. I'm busy." She picked up her pencil and scooted her chair back to the desk, dismissing him with her eyes.

"Like you have been for the last two weeks? Come on, let me buy you lunch. Even busy executives need to eat!" He grinned his calculated, engaging grin. "Besides, I have some new ideas you might be interested in."

"All right, Georgie." Angie sighed resignedly. "One hour. I really am swamped right now."

Georgie stood, fastidiously brushing microscopic particles of fiberfill padding from the seat of his trousers. "Let's take my car," he said in a self-satisfied tone that immediately made Angie regret her decision. "I left the engine running."

LUNCH WAS IN a small deli on the waterfront. It was full of people eating on the run. After waiting nearly half an hour, Georgie flashed a folded ten-spot at the harried waiter, who immediately recalled an empty table on the terrace.

"You haven't changed, Georgie," Angie said, as the waiter preceded them across the tiled floor, smirking like a coconspirator.

"Neither has human nature," Georgie retorted smugly.

Ten minutes into her soup and salad, Angie knew that Georgie's new ideas were just variations of the same old theme.

"Maybe you don't know how much things have deteriorated while you were out playing fisherman...." he began.

"I know exactly how bad things are, and I have a number of plans to put us back on track. And none of them include selling out—to WesPac or anyone else!"

"Oh?" Georgie's eyes again assumed their artless expression. "I wondered if that wasn't the reason you shipped out with Montero's—get something on them, maybe try to make them sweeten the pot?"

"Has anyone ever told you how damned... *disgusting* you can be? If that's the way you do business, I'm amazed that you and your clients have lasted this long! You have no concept of honor or honesty or—"

"In *business?*" Georgie's eyebrows rose incredulously. "Give me a break! That holier-than-thou attitude is just one more strike against Reno's. You may go down *honorably,* but you'll go down just the same. And then what're you going to do? Make your living cooking in the fleet?"

He snorted. "Not likely! I happen to know that the *Sea Witch* wouldn't take you back on a bet!"

Angie glared down her nose at him. "And just *how* do you know that?" she spat out in a chilly voice.

"Come on. Everyone knows everyone in the fleet. I got it from a buddy who has a friend whose brother-in-law used to work on the *Sea Witch.* And he told my buddy that Captain Hernendes says he'd quit before he'd let them put a woman on his boat again. Bad luck, he says—'everyone knows that' he says!" Georgie chortled. "Yeah, for sure, anything bad that happens on the *Sea Witch* for the next ten years, he's going to put the blame on you!"

"And just *who* is Captain Hernendes?" she asked in a voice that had dropped below freezing.

"*Who?*" Georgie snickered unpleasantly. "Alessjandro Hernendes? Short guy? White hair, what there is of it? Mouth like a sewer, but he can find fish?"

He spoke with exaggerated patience, as if he were talking to a slow-witted child. At her blank look, he sighed loudly. "Alessjandro Hernendes, the skipper of the *Sea Witch?* You know, the guy who hired you to sling hash for him?"

"You must be mistaken. The skipper of the *Sea Witch* is Joseph Callais."

"I don't make mistakes like that, Angie." Georgie spoke with his usual patronizing smirk. "It's my job. I've never heard of any Joseph Callais. And I'm telling you, Alessjandro Hernendes is the skipper of the *Sea Witch.* Has been ever since she was launched, back in '82."

"Aw, ANGIE!" Asa Cox wailed. "What difference does it make? You got your trip, you got your money. What d'you care who's the skipper?"

"Asa, you snake, just answer the question!"

"Jeez, you sound just like your mother!" He looked up at her with resentful eyes. An Amazon, Joe had called her. She was that, all right! How on God's green earth had she ever heard about the switch in skippers, anyway? Joe'd have his head! "I'm not supposed to say anything," he whined. "You want to get me fired?"

"I won't tell a soul, Asa. I promise."

Asa exhaled in an explosive sigh of defeat. "Alessjandro Hernendes *is* the skipper of the *Sea Witch*. Just sometimes Joe takes a boat out if a guy needs a little time off. Like last summer, one of Alessjandro's kids got in some kind of trouble, and Joe took the *Sea Witch* out. That's all." He spread his hands helplessly. "He does that every now and again. It's no big deal."

"Why didn't you tell me?"

"Who figured you'd *care?* Hell, Angie, you got to go out, didn't you? That's more than you were going to get if Joe hadn't told me to sign you on!"

"That's it?"

"That's the story. Remember, keep it under your hat."

Angie turned to go, but at the doorway she stopped. "Who's taking the *Sea Witch* out for the winter season?"

"Why, Captain Hernendes, of course," Asa replied, exasperated. "He's her skipper. Isn't that what I just got through telling you?"

After Angie had gone, Asa was uneasy. The season was long past and Joe was back in San Pedro where he belonged—why the hell was Angie asking questions *now?* There was no way he was going to take the blame for this all by himself.

He decided he'd better give Joe a call.

DON'T THINK ABOUT IT NOW, she ordered herself, as she threaded her way down Market Street. *Wait until you get back to the office, get a cup of coffee, sit down, put your feet up. Then it'll make more sense.*

She heard Georgie's voice. *Alessjandro Hernendes is the skipper of the* Sea Witch....

Then Asa's voice. *Alessjandro Hernendes* is *the skipper of the* Sea Witch....

When Angie reached the office, Charlotte had already gone. The dusty venetian blinds admitted the afternoon sun in stripes. The ancient watercooler in the corner had thin stripes of sunlight marching down one side, and from the ceiling a sickly ivy in a macramé hanger turned grateful leaves toward the weak remnants of light.

Angie didn't open the blinds. Neither did she turn on the lights. Instead, she poured a cup of lukewarm coffee from the coffeemaker on top of the file cabinet and sat down in the chair behind her desk. The thin stripes of light were foreshortened, now marching down Angie's face and disappearing into the shadows on the floor.

What does it mean? she asked herself for possibly the hundredth time. She propped her forehead in her hand, staring down into her cup while the coffee it contained gradually grew colder.

I could call San Pedro, her disjointed thoughts continued. *Someone in Montero's headquarters could tell me... he's one of their skippers, after all. I only have to pick up the telephone and call.* Her hand crawled across the desk and stopped halfway.

Could tell me... what?

Why he had lied?

He hadn't really lied, she told herself now, with strict adherence to the facts. She had simply made certain assumptions about him that turned out not to be true, and he hadn't bothered to deny them.

One glaring fact overshadowed all others; if Alessjandro Hernendes was taking the *Sea Witch* out for the winter season, he would be the one in San Pedro overseeing the shakedown cruise and the hiring of the crew. And if Joseph had not been in San Pedro for the past two weeks, he was someplace else. Someplace where he could have been with her if he chose. And he didn't choose.

Angie had never been much good at the games people play. She learned that during the years she'd spent at the university, where everyone seemed to be hopping in and out of other people's beds as if they were majoring in sex and expected a final exam at the end of the semester. Now she wondered if maybe she should have paid more attention, memorized some of the ground rules of relationships the way she had memorized Advanced Algebra.

Angie propped her elbows on the desk and dropped her forehead into her hands, gingerly massaging the heels of her palms against her throbbing temples. She had no idea how long she sat there, but when she looked up, it was to notice that the sun was very low. The stripes of light from the venetian blinds now fell at the bottom of the far wall.

The watercooler burbled, masking the unexpected sound that had first caught her attention.

Then she heard it again, an unexpected knocking at the door. She frowned. "We're closed," she called.

The knock came once more, sharper this time, and accompanied by words that were incomprehensible.

Angie got up and walked to the door. Separating two slats on the blinds a fraction of an inch, she peered into the twilight on the other side.

My mind must be playing tricks on me, she told herself in confusion. The tall figure that filled the doorway was so much a part of her waking thoughts and sleeping dreams that, for an instant, she wasn't sure which she was doing now. In the next instant she threw open the door and flung her arms around his neck.

"Joseph!" she cried, burying her face in his neck with a joyousness that canceled the doubts of the past two hours, as if they had never happened at all.

In one impetuous motion he clasped her in his arms, stepped inside and closed the door with a single, well-placed kick. His body fitted itself to Angie's as expertly as if they had never been apart. His lips found hers and bruised them with a kiss that, when they finally came up for air, left both of them breathless and shaken.

"Joseph," Angie whispered, clinging to his neck, laughing and crying at the same time, "I *knew* you'd come, but where . . . ? How . . . ?"

"Asa Cox called me—"

"Asa?"

" . . . and I grabbed one of our spotting helicopters and flew right down."

"Helicopters?" Angie murmured into his neck. "You fly helicopters? You never told me that."

"There are a number of things I never told you." In the silence of the dim office, his voice sounded flat.

"I know you aren't taking the *Sea Witch* out for the winter season," Angie said. "Is that one of them?"

He let his arms fall from around her shoulders. "In a way. I was a fool to think that it wouldn't get back to you. Yes, that's part of it. But there's more. I hope you'll hear me out."

Angie reached for the light switch by the door and flipped it. She saw that Joseph was wearing a gray jumpsuit of the sort helicopter pilots wore when they flew off the decks of tuna boats, spotting for porpoise; he was also wearing the most desolate expression she had ever seen on his face. His eyes were narrowed guardedly, even more so than when he faced directly into the wind, and his wide, sensual mouth was a tight red gash.

Suddenly she was frightened, not sure if she wanted to hear the words that were responsible for that grim face. "Joseph, what is it?" she whispered; then she corrected herself. "*Whatever* it is, we can work it out. Together. I know we can...."

"I had no right to touch you," the slash of a mouth pronounced, lips barely moving. "I knew that from the start. And I have no excuse to offer—"

"Do you mean because you were the skipper?" Angie laughed unsteadily. "But I wanted it as much as you did. If that was wrong, then we're both to blame!"

"No, there's more." He reached for her hands and clasped them loosely. "I have . . . other obligations."

"But . . . but you're not married!" She was bewildered. "What other obligations could come between you and me?"

"Can you be so sure of that? I haven't been straight with you about a lot of things—that could be one of them."

"Yes, I'm sure," she replied with a certainty that broke his heart. "I know you. I know you couldn't have given yourself to me the way you did if you hadn't been free to do it. Anything else—" She lifted her shoulders in Charlotte's eloquent shrug, dismissing anything else as totally insignificant.

"There *is* something else. And it's both more than that and less than that. You'll have to decide which."

Joseph led her by the hands to the desk nearest the door, then hitched one thigh on the corner of the desk and clasped her hands together in his lap. Standing between his knees, Angie found the magnetism between them almost irresistible, but he kept their joined hands as a barrier, tenuous but inviolate.

His thumbs rubbed back and forth on the ticklish inside of her palms. "Do you remember the first time you came aboard my boat—?"

Angie nodded.

"—and I said that if I had a choice, I wouldn't take on a woman?" At Angie's next nod, he continued, "Well, that wasn't quite true."

"I know."

"You know?"

"Asa told me."

"And what else did he tell you?"

"Nothing, really. Only that..." She tried to recall Asa's exact words that gray and overcast June afternoon. "Things weren't what they seemed, that I should be careful..." Angie looked at Joseph strangely. "What did he mean by that?"

"He meant..." Joseph drew a deep and ragged breath. "He meant that I'm not the person you think I am. I'm—"

At that moment, the doorknob rattled. Both Angie and Joseph looked up, startled. There was the sound of a key in the lock, and the door briskly pushed open.

"Hi, baby. I saw your car and the lights, so I figured you were still here." Her eyes fixed on the lock,

Charlotte withdrew her key and dropped it into her purse.

It must have begun to rain, for she was carrying an umbrella, which she shook vigorously on the doorstep and then closed with a snap. Looking up, she smiled cheerfully at her daughter. "Wouldn't you just know it? I forgot my briefcase and there're some papers I—"

Then her hand stopped midair. The smile froze on her face.

"Mom," Angie began, straightening up and turning toward her mother, Joseph's hand still clutched tightly in hers. "I'd like you to meet—"

Slowly Charlotte lowered her hand to grip the doorknob. Her voice was as glacial as the expression on her face. "Montero."

Chapter Twenty-Three

"Charlotte." Joseph inclined his head gravely.

In an instant Charlotte had assessed the situation. She drew herself up to her full, considerable height. Her eyes were on a level with Joseph's, and her face was an imperious mask of displeasure. "What have you said to my daughter?" The words fell from her bloodless lips like sharp and deadly slivers of ice.

"I've said nothing that wasn't the truth," Joseph replied in a grave and courteous tone. He met her arctic stare. "Would you prefer that I left your office?" he asked in the same courteous voice.

"That is between you and my daughter." Briefly her glance shifted to Angie's stunned face; then with contemptuous dignity, Charlotte turned on her heel and stalked out the door, pulling it shut behind her. Her galoshes shuffled like the vindictive wings of an avenging angel in the dreary tattoo of the rain.

Angie looked at Joseph. "Montero," she said tonelessly. When he didn't speak, she knew that it had to be true.

Joseph's head remained bowed.

"Callais?" she said, in a voice as brittle as breaking glass.

"My mother's maiden name. My middle name."

"You used me."

"No."

"You used me. To get Reno's."

"Angie, no!" Her dull, expressionless voice and her dull, expressionless eyes galvanized him to action. He leapt to his feet and reached for her. "Let me explain!"

Angie backed away, stopping him with her hands raised defensively, palms outward, between them. She felt a numbing, deadening cold, colder even than the fearful chill that had seized her on the *Sea Witch*, the night of the storm.

"Yes," she said. "Explain." Her voice had a numb, cold, dead sound.

Joseph drew a ragged breath. He felt as though his entire life depended on the words he spoke next, but he could think of nothing that made the bald facts sound anything less than...incriminating. "I love you, Angie," he began desperately.

Angie kept backing up, never taking her eyes from him, until she felt her desk behind her; then she continued until she had backed around it and had put it directly between Joseph and herself. Slapping her palms flat on top, arms straight at the elbows, she leaned forward with a tight, mocking smile that was nothing more than a crack in the inanimate void of her face. "Go on."

"It's true that when I hired you, I was thinking about Reno's." Bad beginning. He saw Angie flinch as if he'd struck her.

"I wanted it," he continued doggedly, "and I wanted it while it was still a viable company. I took you on because I thought I could make you see the tuna fleet is no place for a woman. I hoped you'd get so fed up that you'd want out of the whole thing, maybe convince Charlotte to sell. I never expected things to take the turn they did. I..." He hesitated, "Underestimated you."

It *hadn't* been her imagination, then. He *had* been trying from the start to keep her off-balance, trying to guarantee that she'd fail. "How you must have laughed at me!" she whispered.

"I never laughed at you. There was just no way I could tell you who I was. That's the whole point of my going to sea in the first place—to keep my identity a secret so the men will open up around me."

Angie's eyes widened. It all made a perverted kind of sense now. That was the reason behind those restless, searching eyes, darting from face to face all those evenings in the galley, during all those interminable poker games! He'd been spying, as surely as if he'd tapped the crew's telephone conversations, or read their mail!

"And they trusted you!" she hissed, outraged.

"I told you I get the best men and I keep them." The unconscious arrogance in his voice twisted the knives that had already pierced her heart. "That's one of the reasons why. I stay in touch with my men. I understand them. I don't ever want to become one of those hands-off kind of managers who takes the profit and forgets the people."

His voice fell a little, hoping that she'd grasp his underlying meaning. "Just like the old skippers used to do back when our ancestors founded the fleet."

The subtle reference was lost on Angie, or else she deemed it beneath comment. "'The best men,'" she scoffed bitterly. "Sure! One lies and the rest swear to it! Asa Cox—that snake! And Captain Hernendes!

But...but Dominic!'' Her voice faltered. "I never expected this of Dominic...." Too late she understood his veiled innuendos, his vague hints that this skipper was not all he seemed to be.

"Dominic was difficult," Joseph admitted. "He's very loyal to your people. But he knew the trouble Reno's was in. It wasn't hard to make him see that selling was the only option you had left.

"It was harder to convince him that you wouldn't be hurt. He only agreed on the condition that he could be there to keep an eye on you. I know he had his doubts at the last, but what I told him was true—I never meant to hurt you."

Angie's eyes flashed dangerously. "Tell me, how far would you have gone for Reno's? Would you have—" she spat out the word "—*married* me to get it?"

"Angie, please! I'd cut off my right arm before I'd hurt you—"

"Don't...don't keep saying that. You did what you did, and we both know why you did it. Don't insult my intelligence by pretending it wasn't intentional!"

"But it's true. By the time I realized I was falling in love with you, it was too late. I couldn't go back and change things, and I couldn't stop my feelings for you. I was...helpless."

He clenched his teeth over the last word—helplessness was not a condition acceptable to him, and it took all the self-discipline he possessed to force himself to admit to it. "It was hell. I knew that either way I was going to lose. I was a fool to think I could keep you from finding out the truth, but I kept hoping something—anything!—would come up. Then Asa called me today, and I knew I'd run out of time."

"Why did you even bother to come back at all? You were home free. Why didn't you just stay up in San Pedro and wait for me to take the hint?"

"I only went back in the first place to make arrangements about the *Dago Red*," he said quietly. "And to try to think this thing through."

He took a step toward her. She recoiled, and he stopped. "Being on shipboard caught us both by surprise." The reference to that thrilling night on MamaLina's veranda was the last shot of a desperate man. "Surely you must remember that?"

"And I sold you my *Dago Red!*" she breathed incredulously.

Joseph didn't know how to beg. He didn't know how to plead. Both were foreign to his nature and his experience. He could do nothing more than state the facts as he saw them, and he saw that it was not enough.

He raked one hand through his hair in utter frustration. Blast her hardheadedness! Blast that stubborn pride that was so like Long Jack's! And yet…why was he surprised now? He'd known that pride and that stubbornness by reputation before she'd ever come aboard his boat.

He recalled Asa's words: *Hell, Long Jack practically raised her on these docks.* And again: *Looks like her mother right enough, but she's got her daddy's temper.*

You blew it, Joseph told himself with unflinching honesty. You knew the situation, you took the gamble and you lost. You lost.

You lost. And now the only question is, how are you going to get through the rest of your life without her?

"Would you rather I left?" he asked in the same grave, courteous voice he had used with Charlotte.

"Yes. Go! But before you do, let me tell you this. You may have gotten my *Dago Red*, but it's the last thing you'll ever get from me! Before I'd sell to you I'd dismantle every boat and sell it for scrap! I'd take them down to Baja and *give* them to the Mexicans! I'd..."

Joseph waited quietly until she had sputtered to a finish, then turned and walked out of her life. The sound of the door opening and then closing was unequivocal. It was final. It was over.

ANGIE SLUMPED TIREDLY behind her desk. From her window she saw, not the busy Market Street wharf, but the red, dirty backside of another dilapidated old building.

She had moved the corporate offices of Reno Fisheries from their prime location on the wharf to a cubbyhole on the third floor of a rundown brownstone marked for eventual urban renewal. There was only one desk; for now she and Charlotte took turns manning a telephone that never rang.

The winter season had been only marginal. The skipper she had hired to replace Captain Amador on the *Charlotte E.* had been no more than mediocre, unable to get along with either his manager or his crew. He had come to Reno's with lukewarm references, and Angie remembered a time when she would have indignantly sent him packing. But no more. Under her new and irascible skipper, the *Charlotte E.* had done poorly, and the remaining two boats had not been able to make up the difference.

Three months of waiting, three months of hoping, three months of monitoring weather reports as if they were the word of God, trying to determine how the season was going.

It was the last season.

Directly across from Angie's desk, the window looked out at a dentist's office. Dentures While You Sleep his neon sign proclaimed, flashing day and night. The buildings were so close that she could see the patients sitting in his waiting room. She fixed her eye on a long, jagged crack in the crumbling ceiling. It was like Reno's—once a strong and sound structure, carrying the hopes and dreams of generations, now falling into ruin like the stained ceiling of an old, worn-out building.

Joseph had been right, she thought sadly. We lost our rudder when Cappy died, and we've been adrift ever since. It just took us four years to realize it.

Joseph. Her mind came back to him as it always did when she let down her guard. The anger was still there: the unscrupulous way he had stolen her best boat; the way he had just walked out of her life without even a backward glance. She concentrated on anger because it allowed her to ignore the pain. And the humiliation.

She reached across the desk for the stack of bills that were the only thing on top of it, and then stopped. They were no concern of hers any longer.

The decision to sell had been a difficult one. *Whom* to sell to had never been in question. No matter how she felt about its owner, for the sake of the fishermen who depended on her, for the sake of what Reno's once had been, there was only one choice—Montero's.

The papers were drawn up and the contract ready to be signed. The whole thing had been efficiently handled between attorneys—Montero's bevy of high-priced lawyers and the law clerk from the office down the hall representing Reno's, whom Angie had consulted because he was willing and cheap. All that remained to be done was the signing of those papers.

"Why go yourself?" Charlotte had asked. "Let the attorney take care of it. Isn't that what we're paying him for? Montero won't even be there, you know. It'll all be handled by that snazzy law firm he keeps on retainer."

"I know that, Mom. He's taken over so many small companies, what does one more matter?" *Only to me. Only to me.* "It's just that ... I think Reno's deserves a better funeral than a bunch of attorneys will give it. Someone should be there who ... *cares.*"

Charlotte sighed. "Why am I wasting my time? You're as stubborn as your father. I could never do anything with him, either, once his mind was made up...."

Chapter Twenty-Four

Over the top of metal-rimmed bifocals, an unsmiling secretary peered at Angie severely.

"I have an appointment—four o'clock."

"Mrs. de Vasconceles? Yes. You're late." Obviously someone to whom punctuality was next to godliness, she studied Angie with mute disapproval. "Did you have some difficulty locating us?"

Angie glanced at her watch, and saw with a pang that she was, indeed, very late. How unbusinesslike, she thought, for the last business ever to be conducted in the name of Reno's.

"A little," she fibbed. Actually, Montero Maritime's sleek new warehouse hadn't been the least bit difficult to find. It stood out like a beacon among the other, older and smaller buildings in the South San Pedro shipyards. It hadn't been the least bit difficult to find the elevator that carried her directly to the top floor, either, nor the offices, once she got there.

What had been hard was making her body go through the motions when her heart and mind cried *No!* What was harder was being so close to Joseph— why, he could be in this very building right now!—and he not know. Or care.

"But I'm here now," she added, in what she hoped came across as a cool and businesslike tone.

"Yes. Well. We were concerned." Pushing a button on her intercom, the woman announced Angie's arrival, then offered a cool smile. "You may go in, Mrs. de Vasconceles. You are expected."

Angie squared her shoulders. This is it, she told herself. This is the last time you'll be the crown princess of Reno Fisheries. C'mon, let's give 'em a show!

Her heels clicked purposefully on the synthetic marble floor as she turned, carrying the briefcase containing the sales contract, and walked into the lion's den.

THE ROOM IN WHICH she found herself was long and narrow, with a conference table and chairs stretching from one end to the other. Instead of the team of attorneys Angie had expected, there was only one, and he stood with his back to the room, looking out the floor-to-ceiling window at the far end. When Angie pulled the door shut behind her, he turned around slowly.

"Hello, Angie."

Her footsteps slowed and then stopped. "Joseph," she acknowledged stiffly.

"I knew you'd come," he said.

"What are you doing here?"

"The same thing you are, I think." His voice echoed hollowly in the vastness of the room. "Witnessing the end of an era."

"How dare you say that!" The exclamation was only a bruised whisper that caught on the lump in her throat. "You, of all people—*you* have no right to say that."

Joseph turned back to face the wall of glass. "Come over here," he said. "I'd like to show you something."

Because one of them was going to have to move if this thing was going to get done, and it didn't look as though it was going to be him, Angie marched down the narrow aisle of plush carpet toward the glass wall where Joseph stood.

Laying her briefcase on the table, she snapped it open, removed a manila envelope containing the sales contract and extended it to Joseph. When he made no move to take it, she tossed it onto the tabletop with a rigid flick of her wrist. Then she joined him at the window.

The shipyards backed right up to the tide line. Forklifts crawled all over loading docks that extended like concrete fingers out into the oily water. The sound of hammers, saws and heavy machinery drifted upward, audible even in this elegant conference room.

She saw that Joseph's eyes were fixed on some activity in the shipyards. "Look down there," he told her, gesturing toward the men working below.

"That's my new seiner they're building. See that flat deck on top of the bridge? That's a helipad. All the new boats will have them. It'll be a real advantage in finding fish."

"And you'll fly the helicopters?"

"Of course."

"Why are you telling me all this?" she asked, her voice harsh. "It has nothing to do with me."

He shrugged. "I just wanted you to know." Looking up from the shipyard, he focused his attention on a ship steaming across the horizon. "I told you I went to sea for the first time at fifteen. I wasn't much older than that when I understood that I was also ambitious. I wanted more. I worked twenty hours a day to build Montero's into what it is today. Sometimes twenty-four. Sometimes I still do. My life's blood is in this place.''

"I . . . I didn't know that," Angie replied. *Just like Cappy, and his father, and his father before him.* "You must be very proud."

"I am." For the first time since she'd entered the room, Joseph looked directly at her.

He had changed in the three months since she'd seen him. He was thinner. These plush surroundings moderated his irregular profile, subtly civilizing the raw angles of his face. The cleft in his chin looked less scarlike.

The jacket of his three-piece suit hung on the back of one of the conference chairs, and he looked very unlike a fisherman in the pleated slacks, silk tie and buttoned vest he wore. The sleeves of his white shirt were rolled up past his biceps, and Angie could see that the new-penny copper had faded from his skin, leaving only a city-streets tan.

She didn't recognize this elegant stranger. They had been as close as two people could get, so close that one moved inside the other, and still he was a stranger.

"Somehow I never pictured you as a captain of industry."

"Just the captain of a tuna boat?"

"It was a fine thing to be," she said softly. "You were very good at it."

"Well, I was that, first. I hope I'll *always* be that first." He inspected her, taking in the slim wool skirt, the sheer, man-tailored white blouse shadowed by the lacy slip beneath it, the high-heeled pumps that emphasized her height and the long, shapely curve of her calf. Tiny diamond studs sparkled in her ears among the short crop of curls. "You cut your hair."

"Yes." Self-consciously, Angie ran her fingers through the boyish cut that barely cleared her collar.

"I like it."

He didn't sound victorious. He didn't sound like a *conquistador* who had vanquished an enemy. Angie tried to rouse the anger that had sustained her for so long, and found, to her surprise, that it seemed to have deserted her.

"I'm sorry about Reno's," Joseph went on. "I know how hard this must be for you."

"Well, you predicted it." Her tone was brusque. "That should give you a great deal of satisfaction."

"So much so that I would have done almost anything not to have seen it happen."

The kindness in his voice shattered Angie's tenuous self-control. She slumped against the edge of the conference table behind her like a balloon with all the air suddenly let out. "Joseph . . ."

"Yes, love?" The endearment was automatic, and it was obvious that he could have bitten his tongue the instant it left his mouth.

"I want to . . . thank you . . . for taking me out on the *Sea Witch.*" Words were so inadequate! They expressed nothing of her sadness, her disappointment, her bitter regret for everything that might have been. "I learned . . . so much. Not enough to help me salvage Reno's, but maybe enough to make me believe that I did everything I could." *And I learned that I could love again, which I had begun to doubt. . . .*

"I learned something, too. I was wrong about women in the fleet. No man could have done a better job than you did. In the future, all my boats are going to have separate quarters for women." Joseph smiled, the ironic, slightly self-mocking smile that made Angie's heart flip-flop. "The times are changing in more ways than one."

Turning, he picked up the manila envelope she had dropped on the table. "We might as well get this over with," he said. He slid the contents of the envelope onto the table and clumsily shuffled through them. Several sheets slipped through his fingers and drifted unnoticed to the floor.

Watching, Angie realized that Joseph wasn't really reading the contract at all.

"We'd better get Ms. Sandoval in to notarize this," he said, but he made no move toward the intercom.

"Look, Angie," he burst out suddenly. "Would it help you any if I told you that I think you did everything it was possible to do? You used your loan extensions exactly the way you should have to maximize their effect. If the cards hadn't been stacked against you from the beginning, you might even have pulled it off. You—"

Angie's lungs inflated with a short, sharp breath. "What do you know about my loan extensions?"

Joseph's gray eyes immediately vanished into narrow, veiled slits. "Only what everyone else knows," he replied evasively.

"No," Angie said slowly, releasing the breath at a slow, measured rate. "No one knew that, not even WesPac. Only the bank. And you."

She stared at him in disbelief, the truth dawning on her in a sudden flash of insight. "You guaranteed my notes," she whispered. "I should have *known* we weren't getting that money against our future profits.

The bank knew—everyone knew!—that there weren't
likely to *be* any future profits!'' She was dumfounded.
"But... but *why?*"

"Just because I wanted to," Joseph said gruffly, still
not meeting Angie's astonished eyes. "I don't mind
underwriting courage."

"But if I'd sold to WesPac, you would have lost it
all!''

"I didn't think you'd sell to WesPac."

"But... you could have had us months ago," Angie
continued in a bewildered tone. "Without those loan
extensions we were finished. You'd won. I... I don't
understand."

"It was never a question of winning and losing,
love," Joseph said gently. "That's what you didn't
understand."

She looked at him searchingly, as if seeing him again
for the first time. This man, this Joseph, with his un-
swerving integrity—it dawned on Angie in another
sudden flash of insight that he was exactly what she
had perceived him to be from the very start.

He *was* a *conquistador.*

And if he had made mistakes, if he had misled her,
it hadn't been intentional deception, she realized; it was
only due to his lack of experience with subterfuge, and
how could that be bad?

"Joseph," she whispered haltingly, gripping the edge
of the table until her knuckles turned white. His name
tasted sweet on her tongue. It sounded as though it belonged there. But it didn't, not anymore. "I'm sorry.
I'm just so sorry. I was wrong about... so many
things."

"If either of us needs to be sorry, it's me. I should
have been straight with you, right from the beginning

Under the circumstances, you had every right to believe what you did.''

''No, you had to keep your secret. I understand that now. I only wish...''

''What?''

''I wish—'' Her voice was low, and filled with tentative hope, speaking as much to herself as to Joseph. ''I wish we could...start all over again.''

Joseph looked down at her. ''I'm afraid it's too late.''

Angie nodded miserably.

''We've come too far for that.''

She continued to nod, feeling everything that mattered to her slipping inexorably away, and knowing that she had no one but herself to blame.

''But...maybe...we could pick up where we left off....'' Joseph clasped both her hands with his and pulled her toward him, crushing beyond legibility the remaining sheets of the contract that he still held.

Angie noticed other changes. The smell of diesel fuel was gone. So were the fainter odors of perspiration and fish and Old Spice. In their place was a clean smell of soap and an expensive men's cologne. The hands that moved to cup her face were different, too. The calluses—they were gone.

Then the sensations he was evoking made her decide that she loved the new smell and the smoother hands every bit as much as she had the old. And when he wrapped his arms around her with murmured assurances that he would never let her go again, they were the same arms, whether clothed in blue cotton or smooth white silk.

The sounds of the busy shipyard drifted upward. Over Joseph's shoulder, Angie's gaze traveled beyond the glass wall, past the bustling, industrial waterfront, to the San Pedro ship channel, where the sun was setting the stage for one of its more magnificent sunsets. The pure white clouds were backlighted with gold, and pink and orange ribbons streamed across the sky. Fiery red in the west marked the path of the setting sun. The entire horizon was shot with flame.

Angie, descended from seafaring folk on both sides of her family, read the sky without even knowing that she did so. *Red sky at night, sailor's delight.*

Her arms tightened around Joseph's neck. "Promise me, Joseph," she said suddenly and fiercely into his ear, "promise me that you'll always come back to me."

He bent over her, folding his body around her in ways that said love and commitment and forever. And as solemnly as if it were really within his control—the same way Mano had promised, the same way Long Jack had promised, the same way every man who had ever gone to sea promised every woman who stayed behind—he vowed that he would.

Relive the romance...
Harlequin and Silhouette
are proud to present

by Request™

A program of collections of three complete novels by the most requested authors with the most requested themes. Be sure to look for one volume each month with three complete novels by top name authors.

In June: **NINE MONTHS** Penny Jordan
Stella Cameron
Janice Kaiser

Three women pregnant and alone. But a lot can happen in nine months!

In July: **DADDY'S HOME** Kristin James
Naomi Horton
Mary Lynn Baxter

Daddy's Home...and his presence is long overdue!

In August: **FORGOTTEN PAST** Barbara Kaye
Pamela Browning
Nancy Martin

Do you dare to create a future if you've forgotten the past?

Available at your favorite retail outlet.

Take 4 bestselling love stories FREE

Plus get a FREE surprise gift!

Special Limited-time Offer

Mail to Harlequin Reader Service®

3010 Walden Avenue
P.O. Box 1867
Buffalo, N.Y. 14269-1867

YES! Please send me 4 free Harlequin American Romance® novels and my free surprise gift. Then send me 4 brand-new novels every month, which I will receive months before they appear in bookstores. Bill me at the low price of $2.71 each plus 25¢ delivery and applicable sales tax, if any.*That's the complete price and—compared to the cover prices of $3.50 each—quite a bargain! I understand that accepting the books and gift places me under no obligation ever to buy any books. I can always return a shipment and cancel at any time. Even if I never buy another book from Harlequin, the 4 free books and the surprise gift are mine to keep forever.

154 BPA AJJF

Name	(PLEASE PRINT)	
Address	Apt. No.	
City	State	Zip

This offer is limited to one order per household and not valid to present Harlequin American Romance® subscribers. *Terms and prices are subject to change without notice. Sales tax applicable in N.Y.

UAM-93R

©1990 Harlequin Enterprises Limited

Discover the glorious triumph of three
extraordinary couples fueled by a powerful
passion to defy the past in

Lingering Shadows

The dramatic story of six fascinating men and
women who find the strength to step out of the
shadows and into the light of a passionate future.

Linked by relentless ambition and by desire, each
must confront private demons in a riveting struggle
for power. Together they must find the strength to
emerge from the lingering shadows of the past, into
the dawning promise of the future.

Look for this powerful new blockbuster by *New
York Times* bestselling author

PENNY
JORDAN

Available in August at your favorite retail outlet.

Calloway Corners

In September, Harlequin is proud to bring readers four
involving, romantic stories about the Calloway sisters,
set in Calloway Corners, Louisiana. Written by four of
Harlequin's most popular and award-winning authors,
you'll be enchanted by these sisters and the men
they love!

MARIAH by Sandra Canfield
JO by Tracy Hughes
TESS by Katherine Burton
EDEN by Penny Richards

As an added bonus, you can enter a sweepstakes contest
to win a trip to Calloway Corners, and meet all four
authors. Watch for details in all Calloway Corners books
in September.

HARLEQUIN®
AMERICAN ROMANCE®

AMERICAN ROMANCE INVITES YOU TO CELEBRATE A DECADE OF SUCCESS....

It's a year of celebration for American Romance, as we commemorate a milestone achievement—ten years of bringing you the kinds of romance novels you want to read, by the authors you've come to love.

And to help celebrate, Harlequin American Romance has a gift for you! A limited hardcover collection of two of Harlequin American Romance's most popular earlier titles, written by two of your favorite authors:

ANNE STUART— *Partners in Crime*
BARBARA BRETTON— *Playing for Time*

This unique collection will not be available in retail stores and is only available through this exclusive offer.